BURY THIS

Bury This

ANDREA PORTES

a novel

SOFT SKULL PRESS

BERKELEY

Library of Congress Cataloging-in-Publication Data

Portes, Andrea.
Bury This : a novel / Andrea Portes.
ISBN 978-1-59376-535-4
1. Girls—Crimes against—Fiction. 2. Murder—Investigation—Fiction.
3. Michigan—Fiction. 4. Suspense fiction. I. Title.
PS3616.O7887B87 2014
813'.6—dc23

2013026634

ISBN 978-1-59376-535-4

Cover design by Debbie Berne
Interior design by Domini Dragoone

Soft Skull Press
An Imprint of Counterpoint
1919 Fifth Street
Berkeley, CA 94710
www.softskull.com

Printed in the United States of America
Distributed by Publishers Group West

10 9 8 7 6 5 4 3 2 1

For my grandparents, who saved the world,
and for my son, who saved me

Bury This

PROLOGUE

It would be lily white, this snow. On a strange sort of day where the earth and the sky were the same shade of gray.

How funny. He thought later, that in this moment, the thought tumbling through his head had been annoyance with his wife for wasting so much money on those stupid dolls. A doll collection! Collectibles! He told his friends he would eat his face off if any of those fucking things were ever "worth millions someday" or "gonna be worth a fortune" as his wife pled, pondered, prayed.

It was the last thought he would have before he would become forever "the snow plower." Or, better yet, "the snow plower who found her."

Make these branches coal, grabbing down from the sky. What are they eager to clutch? Make these snow prints hurried, and hurried, and rushed. What are they eager to hush?

There he goes following them, now it's a path, a scurry, a brush. Probably nothing but might as well. Into the woods and the grabby grabby trees, greedily waiting to pluck.

A doll collection!

What a hoot. How gaping and stupid, degrading it was, to

think of that time, what, now twenty years ago, when he had looked into his bride's eyes, under that veil, on that altar, and said the words, "I do." If only he'd known about the doll collection. Just one doll. Things might've been different.

Just one doll is what's there in the snow, in the clutter, in the shutter of light, stab stab stab through the trees.

Just one doll. There it is. But there are porcelain fingers and ceramic toes and glass twinkly eyes, unblinking, unblinking. It is, in fact, a girl.

Not a doll at all.

PART I

I t was a silly job, really. Almost no reason to take it. Except. She remembered now, the panic of the paperwork. Forms!

You must fill this one out, and then this one, too, don't forget this here, and we'll need a copy of your driver's license. Also, a contact. In case of emergency. A formality, really.

Struggling to comprehend the form upon form, little boxes in big boxes, sign here, dot here, if you just initial here. She had forgotten, initially, her name. What is my name? (But why should I remember my name . . . ? It's not as if I ever call myself. When was the last time I saw myself across the room and called my name? Never. That's when.) Well. Why should I know my name?

"Beth."

Okay. There it is. That's it, isn't it? The name I seem to inhabit, have been inhabiting this whole time. And yet, to me, a puzzle. It might as well be Mickey Mouse. At least Mickey Mouse I have said more often.

"Last name?"

"Last name Krause."

That is a name my parents have. At least that one's easier to remember. That is not the foreigner staring back at me in the mirror each morning, like Alice through the looking glass.

No, this was the parents' name, and grandparents', too. All these German names. German German German! My name? My name is German Germany. How 'bout that? My name is Sauerkraut Strudel. My name is Pretzel Wienerschnitzel!

She laughed to herself, out loud, in this silence. The receptionist pretended not to hear.

(Now they'll think I'm crazy.)

(Now they'll know I'm crazy.)

Oh, wait, no. That's right. I get to go around in this outfit, this skin. My deception is complete. Here's how I get to squeak through. What they see:

A young girl, almost twenty-two. With a white rat head of hair, albino hair, yes it's a little stringy and washing it takes too long, it hurts my arms, what if someone else could wash it? Honky skin. White as paper. Almost blue. You see, a ghost. I get to be a young-looking sort of ghost with white mouse hair and gray saucer eyes and a stupid little nondescript form skinny and stringy and I'll put a dress on me and no one will know.

No one will know that underneath there are circles and then nipples and a triangle down below. I don't want these circles, never asked for them. They shouldn't be there, I sure as hell don't want them. I should ace bandage them so no one will know. If no one knows then no one will give me that eating look and I am safe. See me in my dress. A french fry with eyes.

This room. Blue and birch with papers everywhere, a

clipboard, a cork board, put a note on it and then you'll remember. Then another and another. "Terry's bake sale, September 5th," "Don't forget to lock up!!," "Drops = 8 PM, 11 PM!," "Toiletry Kits under the SINK! $1 for extras – No exceptions!!!" A convention of exclamation points, as inane as it is urgent.

This desk. Metal but a green sort of metal. Mint green metal. A candy desk. Clunky. Behind the coffee machine, there is Jimmy Carter and his big peanut smile. That jar filled with yellow wrapped butterscotch candies. That half-fridge. Something always smells sour in that half-fridge.

And the receptionist. Well, let's be honest, she's seen better days. Maybe one day I'll look like that? I think she drinks. Maybe here. Maybe underneath that desk in drawer number two is a little flask of Seagram's to take the edge off the day or put the edge on, or just do something, goddammit, to eat these hours, gobble them up. Endless, this life.

"What do you think are your qualifications?"

A ridiculous question. The woman, bright blonde, it doesn't match her face, and brown eyes. Her hair must be black for God's sake. A sea-foam green sweater jacket, there's a tie, a sweater at the waist and she is bundled up. A little bundle of brisk blonde beauty, fading, but yes, she would find company, at the tail end of happy hour, there she would be, at that hour, or later, a find. A virtual treasure.

"Excuse me?"

"Your qualifications? What do you think qualifies you to work at the Green Mill Inn?"

I mean, you might as well laugh in her face.

Well, ma'am . . . and I do use that term loosely . . . I believe I am qualified to work at this shithole because I have nothing better to do and I'd like to have some money around for a change and maybe disappear from my parents a few hours a week to something other than choir practice at St. John's Presbyterian.

"I'm a real people person!"

Banana blonde feigns interest.

"'Sides that I'm a real quick learner and I took a typing class at Hope, fifty-five words per minute. Not that I'm bragging or anything."

"I see. Well, you won't have to do much typing here, Miss . . . "

"Krause."

"Miss Krause. This is mostly just taking reservations, signing in guests, making sure the front bathroom is clean . . . you don't have to clean it, Janelle does that. Just making sure it's nice and there's toilet paper and, sometimes, it's nice to have a candle or Glade freshener, just if you want it. It's mostly your bathroom, after all, customers rarely use it. But, if they do, you know, it's the first thing they see, so, you want it to look nice. Professional."

Mind-numbing, this monologue, ode to a well-stocked bathroom, applesauce through a sieve. And now the mere facts, now rattled off like gunfire, too quick, can't catch it.

"Open at five. Close at one. One-hour break for dinner. You can take a fifteen-minute break every few hours, but, really, the whole job's like a break. Between customers. So might as well stay here, in case the boss drops by. Coffee's in the cabinet, Folgers, you gotta make it. There's Styrofoam cups for customers, if they ask.

Creamer, sugar, Sweet 'N Low. You can put out cookies. Maybe at Christmas. Makes it festive, ya know. See ya Monday."

She refastens her belt, a point made in sea foam.

"I got the job?"

"Yeah . . . oh, silly me. Of course. You got the job." And then, an unconvincing smile.

"Congratulations."

TWO

Shauna Boggs had never thought about what she was doing, and what she was getting paid for. Or, at least, she'd never let herself think about it. That was something for grasping of steering wheels and late-night drinks alone in front of the TV.

You could drink and drink and watch that late-night chatter a thousand times. Clink. Clink. Clink. And then, at some point, what, sleep? Or was it blacking out? She couldn't tell anymore. The whole thing was so far-fetched. So far away from what she'd planned for herself, like raindrops on the windshield.

This wasn't her knight. Nor her pawn. Nor was she the queen. No, certainly not. Driving home in her beige Chevy Impala, knuckles clasped around the wheel, driving forward into the drink, or the hope of the drink. She could almost believe that it was not her. Here in this car. On this night. Who had just done that.

It was funny how she always took a shower after. Sometimes the guy, the date, the not-John, would say, "Why do you always take a shower after?" She, if she could've said it, if she were free . . . she would've said, "Because I hate you. I hate everything about you. Your black eyes and your black hair and the stuff you put in it and your hairy everything, belly, back, ass, and the thought of you, the look of you, the seeing of you above me moving up down up down grunt grunt grunt, transferring myself into the walls. Because I have to wash you off me, you dumb sonuvabitch. What do you think? Look at yourself?! Why don't you take a good goddamn guess as to why I always take a shower after?! Jesus!"

It's not fucking calculus!

But no, she would say, instead, "Oh, you know, I'm old-fashioned I guess . . . "

Old-fashioned.

Ha. That's a laugh. I am old-fashioned enough to let you fuck me and then drive away in my beige Chevy Impala, with white snot on my belly and a hundred and fifty dollars in my pocket and a mouth full of thirst that can never be quenched, will never be quenched, again.

Look at it this way. At least she wouldn't have to work at that suck-ass job like perfect-face. The Green Mill Inn. What a dump. There wasn't a mill around for miles, never had been.

No, leave that kind of work to little miss Goody Two-shoes who sings in the choir.

THREE

Omaha Beach was almost a pigfuck. Near sacrilege to say, but something Lt. Colonel Charles Krause ran over again and again in his head, trying to get it right. The sheer randomness of it all, or had it, in fact, been perfectly right. Divinely right.

Heading on a bobbing cork into that squall, next to him Private First Class Dwyer puking into the chop-chop sea. Jesus, could they have picked a better day? On the other side, Private First Class Solano praying quietly, solemnly, you wouldn't even know he was praying . . . just whispering to himself really. Then ahead. That stretch of beach. Low tide. Christ. Whose idea was that?

But it was all thought out. Half an hour before the B-17s had flown over and bombed the fuck out of the Germans. So they were told. When they got there, they would stroll along that low-tide beach, meet each other in the grass above and, who knows, maybe kill a few straggling Germans, vicious fucks. Isn't as if they don't deserve it. The motherland. What a crock.

But the metal bobbing cork, halfway between the sip and the shore, is witnessing no strolling, no meeting. No, no such luck.

It's a fucking shooting gallery.

Three hundred yards of beach and it's a fucking shooting gallery. Sitting ducks. The air strikes missed.

A half hour.

A half hour for these sick fuck Germans to wake up and drink their whatever the fuck they drink and wait for us, US, like sitting ducks on the low-tide beach.

Better jump off the side now, better jump off the side of the bobbing metal cork—Jesus, they are mowing 'em down in front like a firing squad. Might as well be back in the American Revolution over here.

Jesus.

Ratatat-tat.

"Jump!"

"But that's not the—"

"Jump, goddammit!"

Now it's motherfucking ice cold, all the way up to the chest, this pack, these boots, this gun, this fucking thing is never gonna fire. If I make it.

Now bullets through the water. Pshew pshew pshew. Jesus. There and there and over there, too. Now blood, Jesus. Seeping out everywhere—how strange it goes, little tentacles, clusters. It's not my blood. It's not my blood yet.

Now is the worst part. The waters ending. Now the shore. The shore. Oh, Christ. How many men? It's crowded. This is a fucking crowded party, my friends. And these are my friends, indeed.

Stay down. Stay down.

OK.

You can do this. Just a stretch of beach, just a stretch of beach. Bulletproof. I am bulletproof. I'm an American and this is how I save the world.

When you look at the aerial shots of Omaha Beach on this day, you will get confused. There ocean. Yes, familiar. There's sand. Yes, that seems right. There is the grass above and the bunkers. Yes, I understand.

But then, below, where the ocean meets the shore, there are all these skinny rectangles, one, two, three, even four skinny rectangles parallel to the beach. All along the length of the beach. Hundreds of them.

And then, above, one, two, three, even four above of the skinny rectangles, perpendicular to the beach, up a ways, on the shore. The length of the beach, as well.

This is, say, one hundred yards of beach. Not much. It's a big goddamn beach, you could only get so much in one goddamn photo.

And the skinny rectangles?

Make the skinny rectangles parallel to the beach, floating willy-nilly but more or less beached by the ebb and flow of the tide . . . make them the ones dead in the water. Private First Class Dwyer, who had been vomiting in the metal cork. Private First Class Solano, who had whispered to himself a prayer. Did he whisper it there in the water, too, did he whisper it to the sand and the blood in the tentacle pattern ebbing to and fro, to and fro?

And perpendicular? Make those rectangles injured and hidden up against the dunes. Make those the ones that got grabbed and dragged and hauled and left. Make them live. Most of them.

Make one of them a man named Charles Krause. A man who, seeing his feet below him and the skinny rectangles floating in the water ten yards down, would think now, would always think, he was not a man for getting injured. He was not a man to be torn to pieces by bullets, but the bullets begged to differ, bleeding him out into the brine. Leveled. He should've been up there fighting. He should've made it up the sand. It was a guilt he carried with him from that day to the next day to the next year and to the rest of his days, back in Michigan, Muskegon, Michigan—where he would never tell a soul. No one. Not even his wife.

FOUR

The snow plower would never be upset with his wife for her dumb stupid doll collection again. In fact, the first thing he would do after that day, that long day of questions and more questions . . . looking at that body, waiting for hours, those grueling sessions recounting over and over his every step, movement, thought. The watch on his wrist. The hat in his hand. Everything he had on from that day, he would put in a plastic bag and bury deep dark deep in the back of his closet.

The first thing he would do upon seeing his wife, his sweet, ashy, thankless wife. He would walk up to her, slowly, and crash her up against the wall. He would put his mouth on her shoulder. Flowers on her apron. He would stand her up against the wall and whisper to her deep, "I am stupid. I am a stupid man. Don't ever leave me. I will buy you a doll every day for the rest of your life and build a new room for all the dolls in the world. Stay with me. Just. Stay with me."

At night, his eyes in the ceiling, he would stare back at those ice doll eyes, that porcelain face, and, underneath them, a blue-and-white locket, a cameo. Wedgwood.

FIVE

Shauna Boggs was daddy's little girl. Even though he called her plumpish and sometimes ignored her altogether, she was still his one and only. She knew.

She knew it just like she knew, the day her mom took off, that she was now the lady of the house. It was up to her. She would do the cooking and she would do the cleaning and she would press his shirts and make his Maker's Mark just how he liked it, not too much ice, but not too little either.

She held her position with honor and grace from seven to ten to twelve to fourteen. She held her position as the lady of the house with the seriousness of a librarian.

And when Mr. Boggs came home one night, too late from the Jewel Box, and swooped her up from her bed and carried her into his bed and treated her like the lady of the house . . . she held that position too.

SIX

A police description can look like this: "Body was found at approximately 7:15 AM on March 13, 1978, off Route 31, two miles south of the corner of Pioneers and the Route 31 interchange. There were numerous lacerations to the neck, shoulders, face. Heavy bruising around the wrists and ankles. Blunt force trauma to the skull. Possible death: strangulation."

A police description cannot look like this: "I couldn't see it. I didn't want to see it. How young! How desecrated! How beaten! And then tossed by the side of the road. Discarded trash. A disposable bag. This could've been my daughter, my wife, my niece. Who are they? I will find them. I will find them and I will kill them."

It could say: "Lacerations around the hands and shoulders, defensive wounds, red marks around the wrists and neck, blunt force trauma, possible strangulation."

It could not say: "I have seen that throat in chapel choir, those vocal chords, now silenced, singing in a soprano voice, a voice, quite literally, just like the cliché, like an angel. But how can you not think it? A voice, yes, like an angel, in the chapel choir. There, on the altar, singing 'Ave Maria.' A soprano voice, a stunning voice, singing 'Look Homeward Angel,' singing 'Dona Nobis

Pacem,' singing 'All Things Bright and Beautiful' and even, on a lighter day, 'Southern Cross.' 'This Little Light of Mine.' A child's voice. A child's face. A doll face."

It could say: "Body, half-clothed, facing ground. Dress, torn. Remnants of a sweater. Necklace. A Wedgwood cameo."

It could not say: "I have seen her in that sweater on the way to school, on the way to St. John's, in the line at the Farmer Jack, in the line at the Community Shores. I have seen that sweet thinning baby blue sweater with the butterfly, or was it a flower, on the collar. I have seen that robin's egg sweater as Beth Krause walked with her father, Lt. Colonel Charles Krause, a war hero, by the shore of the lake. I have seen her clutch that Wedgwood locket, a self-conscious shrug, at school, at choir, at Hope."

It was these thoughts, all of these thoughts, that tumbled, rattling through the head like pickaxes, of Samuel Christopher Barnett, Detective Barnett, not yet five years on the force. A decent man. A kind man. Tried to be kind anyway.

Oh, believe me, there were a million other things his pulse was urging him to do other than write down little words in little boxes, checks and more checks, here and there, on forms and more forms. A traffic ticket for a corpse.

There were a million terrorizing, shocking, blindsiding impulses but no . . . there he was, pen in paper, Detective Samuel Barnett. Brown mouse hair. Skinny no matter what. Old-timey Keystone Cop face. No one looked like that anymore. And he would've done them, every million of them, had he not had to, what is it, "keep a brave face," "stand tall," for the cameras.

And there were cameras. You betcha. For a band the length

of a football stadium, up and down the sliver of that Michigan lakeshore stretch, there were little white boxes with tires on them, barely visible in the snow. Camouflaged. And out of each of these boxes came one, usually a lady, in a smart, snappy getup, with a black penis stick in her hand you were supposed to talk into. A microphone. Careful what you say. Easy now.

That little stick and those batting eyes can get a lot out of you but you better be careful. Brace yourself as the first one comes barreling forward, and then another and another. An army of smart-dressed swine.

Brace yourself. Easy there, Sammy.

"Detective, is the victim a local? Is the victim female or male? What age? Do you consider foul play? Is there a suspect? Do you have a motive? Is the—"

An army of swine. A murder of crows.

Peck peck peck.

What did they want from him? Hadn't they had enough? They had a blood-red slab of girl-meat in the snow. Wasn't that enough? Brisk. Brisk. Be brisk. Don't let them know.

"The body is yet to be identified. No further questions."

But then, in the back, a yelp. "Here's the snow plower! Here's the guy who found her! I got him! I got him!"

And then, the parade goes thataway and Detective Barnett stands still in the snow, abandoned. Put your feet in the snow, look up to the sky. Ask the trees to wonder why.

SEVEN

Shauna Boggs played a game on Beth Krause once that wasn't a game at all. Shauna knew the game, though, she'd learned it well. She'd had it played on her.

It was an after-school sort of game that started with playing dress-up. When Shauna first learned to play this game she was in the seventh grade and didn't mind looking in the mirror and playing dress-up in Mommy's clothing 'cause Daddy said it was okay. Encouraged her even.

"Here," he would say. "Try this."

And she would try this, and she would giggle and say, "Oh, no, not me" or "Oh, maybe . . . someday." If it was something fancy. Something fancy from Mommy, before she left. Before she died? No . . . she didn't die, Shauna. She left. She left because of you.

Her mom, before she left, had a menagerie of looks, from sophisticated to prim to downright slutty. Too many clothes for that little closet. Too many clothes for that little house. Guess that's why she left.

Her mom, Shauna's mom, was from Niagara Falls. The good part. The part up above the falls with long stretches of houses and even longer stretches of lawn. Why she'd ever married Troy Boggs was beyond anyone, including her, which is why, one day, looking around at the pale lead house, which could've used a coat of paint, and almost could've been the home sweet home she thought she'd been looking for, she simply made a calculation. It was a math problem. What times what makes me stay? Versus . . . what times what makes me go? What is my opportunity cost? Of course, there's the girl. Well, I can't take her with me now, can I? Then I really wouldn't have a chance.

(What kind of fella's gonna grab up a pretty lady and a kid? I'll tell you what kind. A loser. That's what kind.)

No, Shauna's mother had no intention of landing herself a loser. Another one, anyway. Once was enough. Although. Troy had been cute, sexy in a sinister sort of way. She liked the way he fucked her at least. That was one thing he could do. About the only one.

A math problem. Yes, there were some unknowns. Some variables. But still . . . that's what variables were for, wasn't it? The unknown. It was inevitable, really. The minute she'd walked down the aisle, she knew it. Not having her family there. And that tuxedo!

No, Troy Boggs was not the end of the line for her. She'd made a mistake. That's all. Wrong answer. Nothing that couldn't be fixed. And she did fix it. She did. How easy. Easy as putting one delicate foot in front of the other and making her way, tippy-toe tippy-toe, out the door and nevermore.

"Here," Troy Boggs said to his daughter. "Try this."

And this was a dress Shauna Boggs dare not try on. Are you kidding?

"No," she said, pleading. "I can't."

Seeing in her eyes that scared little girl he wanted to protect punch kill fuck, he grabbed her closer, tucked into his arm. "It's okay, honey. Daddy's here. Daddy wants you to."

And so there she goes, little Shauna, out the door and some crumpling and crinkling until, finally, there she emerges from the closet, what a sweet little thing, what a delicate little thing, what a warm, white thing to sink your teeth into.

There she is, little Miss Shauna Boggs, the plump little brunette Michigan beauty standing there, fumbling, not proud or pretty, fumbling silly pig . . . in her mother's oh-so-sophisticated wispy white wedding dress.

She'd left it behind. That bitch. She'd left it behind just as she'd left Shauna behind and she'd left Troy behind. Trash. Trash Boggs. That's a better name for you.

But he'll show the bitch, that la-di-da bitch from Niagara fucking Falls, he'll show her 'cause Troy Boggs gets the last laugh here 'cause Troy Trash Boggs gets the last laugh now by lifting up his daughter's skirt, your daughter's skirt, in your oh-so-pretty wispy white dress.

EIGHT

Detective Samuel Barnett had had enough of these goddamn interviews. Every two seconds it seemed that black stick was in front of him, asking him questions, that glass circle with cameraman attached, asking now more questions, questions about his questions. Interviews about his interviews.

Already he'd had the family, the church, the classmates, the Green Mill Inn staff, the hotel guests, some union guys, the entire chapel choir and now, this, finally, inevitably, the best friend.

Walking down that gray slit of a path, that patch of a lawn, to that paint-peeled farmhouse, he was dreading the interaction. He'd left all interaction with his own girls to his wife, years ago. Lady stuff. He didn't know how to, nor did he want to know how to, talk to young girls. Just leave them be. Somehow, he thought, that was all you could do.

He hadn't expected the little girl to answer anyway. Even his knock was unwilling. Too bad for him, his knuckles made it to the door, the door concurred and opened.

Dammit. But no. Not out loud.

Keep it professional.

She is tiny like Beth. She is Beth's age. She is shaking somehow.

"Excuse me, Miss, I am looking for Shauna Boggs . . . is that you?"

Silence.

"Yessir."

"Well, okay, then. My name's Detective Barnett. I'd like to ask you some questions, if you don't mind."

"DA-AD!"

The screen door can fly at you if you're not used to getting it slammed in your face. Step back. Step back. Easy there. Take things slow. The girl's probably traumatized.

Troy Boggs. Yes, I know him. Just like I knew it was you, Shauna. It's okay. I know your mama left. Everyone in town knows that dirge. Poor thing.

"It's okay, Miss Boggs . . . Shauna…I'm just here to ask a few quick things. Won't take a minute."

The way Troy Boggs shades his way into sight, you'd think he was there all along, just idling. Like the light changed and there he was.

"Sir."

"Yes, sir. Mr. Boggs. Sorry to bother you. I just have to ask a few questions. Routine. About the . . . incident. I'd like to ask your daughter. If that's all right with you."

Quiet house. Empty house. No-mom house.

"Officer, we'd be happy to help. Anything. I just wish I had something more to offer you, something to drink maybe? Some saltines maybe?"

Open the screen door goes and now the little cluster moves

inside. It's a pale-yellow kitchen, what could be the sweetest of kitchens, but not anymore.

It's a card table in the middle and some metal chairs, one plastic. Troy Boggs dusts off the head chair for the officer, sits down his daughter and takes a seat beside her, concerned.

"Shauna, do you remember the last time you saw Beth Krause?"

Silence.

That little brunette sure knows how to stare at the ground.

"Approximately?"

"Yes. I saw her on her way to work. She was coming back from practice at St. John's. I tried to get into that choir but, I guess I didn't have the voice, so . . . "

"So, she was coming back from choir practice, back from St. John's Presbyterian?"

"Yessir."

"Do you remember where, exactly?"

"On Spring Street, past the Farmer Jack."

"Okay, good. That's good, Shauna."

It was funny looking at this girl. What was she . . . eighteen, nineteen, twenty, maybe twenty-one? It was like she was locked in time. Strange. You would never take her for more than fifteen. Even her gestures were childlike. Flinching. Samuel thought about his two middle-school girls bounding down the stairs, buzzing, stampeding toward their dinner, snickering, talking about God-knows-what. But this girl. This girl made of glass. A reed ready to snap.

And poor Troy. There next to her, troubled. A tear in his eye. You could tell he was shook up, too. Well, hell, why wouldn't he be? If it were my daughter's best friend I'd have them both put in a tower by now. Lock 'em up and throw away the key.

"She was real rushed, you know. Said she was on her way to work."

"At the Green Mill Inn . . . is that right?"

"Yessir."

"And did she call you or did you hear anything from her since, from the Green Mill Inn?"

"No, sir."

"Nothing?"

"No."

Now she is putting her head down and her father is putting his hand on her shoulder. Oh, God, please don't break down in front of me, Troy Boggs. You're a grown man!

Shauna looks up from the bottom of the world.

"Mister. She was the sweetest girl I know. Just real kind. She didn't deserve this."

Detective Barnett knows his lines well.

"Miss Boggs, no one knows why or how any of this happened but you can rest assured of one thing. We'll find who's to blame."

"That's right, honey." Troy Boggs holds his daughter square on the shoulders. Such a good man. Such a good father. What with his wife leaving him and all.

NINE

You could make a funeral here today. With the sky bright blue for miles, the rolling green lawn, on and on, never mind the tombstones. You couldn't have picked a better day.

It's a hole in the ground. Nine by four. Around it are the tops of people's heads. Black hats. The chapel choir is there, too. At the service, back at St. John's, they'd sung "Walk with Me Lord" and "Dona Nobis Pacem." Now, here on the lawn, Beth Krause sang at her own funeral. The conductor from the chapel choir dutifully, quietly, pressed PLAY on the tape recorder and there she was.

Even when she was alive, the timbre of that voice, the pale white-haired girl bellowing out the "Ave Maria" to such great heights, even then, it had been hard for the stoniest of hearts to "keep a grip," to "maintain" as it were. Such a thrilling voice from such a shy, tepid girl. A girl in a baby blue sweater with, what was that? A bow? A butterfly? A tiny little piece, a minuscule piece, of vanity. Maybe it was a dragonfly. A cameo behind it.

But now, here, with the chapel choir standing to the side and the service over, with Lt. Colonel Charles Krause and his wife, Dotsy, the two of them standing there, stoic, the voice coming out of the tape recorder, Beth Krause singing at her own funeral, might as well have been made of tears. The girls, Shauna and her friends, were shaking uncontrollably, sobbing themselves into convulsions. Even Troy Boggs had to stand them straight. Please, girls, please. Oh Lord. Stand still.

The chapel choir, twenty-six of them, simply stood stooped in tears, a row of weeping willows, unabashed.

It was a wonder to think, looking on that little hill in Muskegon, Michigan, on that big blue day in mid-winter that the hill itself wouldn't cleft itself somehow from the land around it and float downstream on a river of tears, down to the Ohio, and then the mighty Mississippi, down to the warmer climes where there is no snow to find a girl.

It was a wonder, too, to think as the "Ave Maria" split the sky in twain and the hearts and faces off the gathering of what must've been the entire town, that the only two faces laid blank, laid bare, were that of Lt. Colonel Charles Krause and his handsome wife, Dorothy.

PART II

What would it all mean, that Technicolor rush, that parade of technology, a mad dash into the future, ahead of what, exactly? What was being kicked into the past backward, impatient to drink, what future? And then, that sunny sunny morning, that dirty killing plane, that towering cloud of dust. Then the second, its mean little twin, flying willful, a fire wrath, a great gasping horror, an innocence felled. What would become of it? Who would succeed, who would collapse, and who would follow? What world would we have to save now? Two thousand three and the cards had been dealt but the hand had yet to be played.

And now, this new breed. Born after *Star Wars*. A litter of consumers, giddy-grasping.

But some of them were not so simple. Look at Katy. She had joined Spring Youth in the summer of 2002, mostly for the skiing. There were two trips to Mammoth, Colorado. One in fall. One in spring. Never mind that it was a Christian group. That wasn't the point. The point was that it was the only way to get to those powdery Colorado slopes from Muskegon, Michigan, twice a winter for next to nothing.

Yes, they sang Christian songs at the meetings. She actually liked that part. She especially liked "Southern Cross."

"When you see the Southern Cross for the first time . . . "

Those folksy lyrics, the guitar twang. It didn't seem harmful, sinister, or any of the other things her sister rolled her eyes about. Who cares about God. Katy never thought about it. Although sometimes she wondered where He had been that crisp sunny morning in September, two years earlier. No one knew what to make of it. And, to be quite honest, she did think some of the lessons from the Bible-study book were good lessons. Love thy neighbor. Well, you couldn't argue with that, now, could you?

So, when the head of the Spring Youth, Muskegon, chapter insisted she apply to Hope College on a Christian Youth scholarship, she didn't blink. What was wrong with that? These were good people. A couple of them were a little scrambled, but for the most part, these were kind, modest people. People who baked banana bread.

When Katy won the scholarship to Hope College, mid-June, she was whirling with excitement, didn't think twice about landing straight on the honors list and maybe more. That's the way things happened for Katy. Quiet, pragmatic, redheaded Katy with wavy hair and green imploring eyes.

She didn't notice, much, the attention in her Film & Television seminar from Brad or Lars or Danek. Even though it was obvious. Anyone could see it. You would have to be a complete imbecile not to see them all circled around, leaning in, facing her.

Film & Television 101 was not in the curriculum, by any means, but Katy had a yen to learn documentary filmmaking and travel the world to places with exotic names and somehow save everyone.

Brad, Lars, and Danek took the class because Katy did.

Brad, tall and spindly. Lars, short with sandy mop hair. Danek, dirt-haired, glasses, and smarter than Hope itself. It was clear Danek was destined for greatness, even with his funny little glasses, one day you would see him in *The New York Times* perhaps. An article maybe. But for now, the three freshmen, along with their beloved Katy, sat listening to Professor Wishik's theory of film, which didn't so much amount to a theory as a concoction of thoughts, thrown in a pot, boiled up and served as a stew. Oh, Professor Wishik. You really were behind the times.

This fluorescent room, these blue chairs with metal legs, these white beech laminate tables, everything plastic and pale, a gutless kind of learning place, dry as chalk.

Somehow through the draining drone of facts and names and titles came an assignment.

Find a subject. Make a documentary. Simple enough.

Now Katy leans in, as do Danek, Brad, and Lars, as the quest is taken up.

Danek says it, almost out of the blue. The others talking, distracted.

"That Krause case."

A lean in, a pause.

"That Krause case. From the '70s. That girl. You know, the one that went here."

Brad and Lars stay silent, taking their cue from Katy. She will make the decision.

"The dead girl?" Katy doodling, somewhere else.

"Yeah. The Hope student."

Silence.

"It's an unsolved case. They never solved it." Stupid. That's what unsolved means, Danek kicks himself. Katy turns him into a dolt, tongue-tied. If only he could get her alone sometime, out of the way of this mediocre audience. Maybe he could introduce her to his parents.

"I dunno." Lars had something more sunny in mind, maybe a documentary about snowboarding.

"No, you know. I think we should. It's got everything. And it's all here. We could do the research ourselves. Interview the people." Katy now up from her notebook, quick, animated.

"Um. Wasn't that like twenty-five years ago?" Lars sees Aspen in his future. A History of Snowboarding. They would start with skiing and move on. He would research. Vail. Steamboat.

"They're still here. The parents. Live down on Rose." Danek nudges, sees a win coming.

Silence. Brad draws in his notebook, waiting for the verdict, apathetic.

"Oh, I love it! Can we? Can we please?" Katy leans in to Brad and Lars, pleading.

The boys look at each other. She has no idea, does she? How they think of her when they turn out the lights. It's silly, almost. Is she blind? They'd kill Professor Wishik himself and boil him in a pot if she said so. Not understanding why. Maybe it was the fact she didn't care so much. How she said marriage was stupid and had yearnings to travel the world by herself. By herself! A girl by herself in Bali! India! Singapore! What a funny girl she was. Independent. Giddy. What would become of her?

Danek settles in, a victory. "Of course we can. I mean, if you guys want to."

Just some stupid assignment. Coulda been anything. Coulda tossed a coin and it'd turn out different.

TWO

"Twenty-five years from 1978 to 2003. Twenty-five years wherein, you name it. Computers. A personal computer. A laptop. An Internet. An email. A new thing, called Friendster. A newer new thing, called Myspace, burbling. A 'social network,' whatever that was. A phone in the car. A mobile phone the size of a brick. Now a cell phone. A cell phone that takes a picture. A cell phone that takes a picture and sends it to your friend . . . in London. Yes, folks, twenty-five years."

Danek pauses.

"If twenty-five years can discover the Internet, the cell phone, this thing the iPod, can twenty-five years discover the secret of a girl murdered, abandoned, by the side of the road?"

He likes his introduction. He finds it provocative.

On the way out to Rose Heights, the furthest thing from his mind was any sort of emotional impact probable here. Danek was not an emotional person. And PS: He didn't believe in Christ either. That was a fantasy. A fairy tale. Something cooked up to tame the masses. Poor-people solace. That all existed so the have-nots wouldn't cut the throats of the haves. What a trick.

Yes, he went to Hope College and yes it was a Reformed

Church school. But Danek was too smart for all that. Fine, believe in your fairy-tale magic. I'll take my degree, GRE, my valedictorian address, my effusive letters of recommendation, my 4.0 average, and shuffle off to graduate school someplace with an actual fucking name. Cornell. Johns Hopkins. Maybe Princeton.

What will happen to all you people? Will you stay here? The thought alone filled him with dread. He shuddered to think, would not let himself think, about the myriad curses that would have to befall him to land him forever . . . here.

Maybe he would come back for Katy and put her in his big mansion back East. They would decorate the Christmas tree together and she would make eggnog and he'd drink and fuck the daylights out of her and she would never, ever think of Brad or Lars or anyone else from this piss-hole pot because he would own her. It would be a Tudor house. A wreath on the door. A dog. Maybe a Lab. Chocolate.

These were the thoughts circling, dizzy, through Danek's brain as they pulled up to 2226 Rose Avenue, the home of Lt. Colonel Charles Krause and his kindly wife, Dotsy.

THREE

It wasn't long before she realized she could stop a room by walking into it. Dorothy Elizabeth Burke. Dotsy. No, she probably shouldn't have come to New York, being a kid from the sticks and all—Odessa, Texas, to be exact.

She was a painter, for God's sake. She was a painter and this was the last of the '40s and New York City was the place to be. A whir of excitement. Christ, she couldn't let it pass her by.

And with that kind of talent, it was only a matter of time, she had her finger on the pulse. Her teacher, Mr. Kaufman, told her he'd seen nothing like her paintings. They spoke of landscapes of the mind. Dreamscapes, he called them. And often, he pointed her out in class. "Let's look at Dorothy's interpretation." No, it wasn't work. It was interpretation. That's how far ahead of them she already was. Her classmates would mutter under their breaths, but it was true, wasn't it? Anyway, it seemed to come easy to her, a fearless kind of talent, almost chance.

At first, walking into a bar, restaurant, club, it had been frightening for Dorothy, all the attention. The venal undressing. The outright staring, goddammit. But, met with a shy cowering, however real, somehow made it worse. No, she couldn't let herself cower. She learned, instead, take a step in, stop, give 'em a second, then eyes to the ground and sideways to the bar. Make bashful coy.

By the time she would reach the bar, there would already be at least three of them, swarming, scowling, vying, chest to her, hearts to her, plotting to get in there.

She was not pretty, nor sweet, nor cute. She was, quite simply, a drop-dead, stop-traffic gorgeous, ink-haired, green-eyed beauty with alabaster skin and bone structure Veronica Lake would envy. And those lips, almost obscene. Sweetheart lips. Kill-you lips. That girl knew how to pout.

She, in fact, knew all the tricks. She was a quick study. Sure, she was just some hick from Odessa, Texas, but that didn't mean she couldn't open a magazine and copy a picture, a hairstyle, a sigh. That didn't mean she couldn't look at Rita Hayworth in a too-tight sweater and say, yes, I see, I see how you do that. And, all of these things, her calmed-down but sometimes disarming small-town-girl accent, her rarely used but sometimes essential provincial ways, in combination with her kill-yourself good looks, made her, instantly, agonizingly, unforgettable, and, ultimately, irreplaceable.

The painting just made it worse. That she was talented . . . a final blow.

And so it would've been, would've gone, until she'd end up celebrated in the Met or cherished on Park Avenue or possibly both . . . . . until she met Edward.

Edward.

For years after, the name alone could make her gulp and grab the nearest cocktail.

It was funny how she met him. How he saw her across the bar. Make no mistake, she liked to drink. Dotsy was out, every night, a drink in one hand, a cigarette in the other, from the day she got to New York to the day she left. She burned it down. Dotsy was not going to let life get away without her. She wasn't going to miss the party. She was the party.

Seeing her across the bar, surrounded by admirers, he could only smile, that first time. A knowing sort of smile. I'll get you. Don't you worry. I'll get you, my pretty.

And then, weeks later, at a party downtown, there she was again. This time in red. Well, why not, it was Christmas season, why not wear red? And wasn't she radiant. A red felt dress. A crimson ribbon bow. Was the dress the present or was she? A wink of a dress, a siren number.

It was that night they would consider their first night. Not that it amounted to much. No sleeping, or even leaving, together. But it was that night they both knew. It was obvious.

This was trouble.

How horribly and blissfully and careeningly they fell in love. Catapulting themselves to a world far, far above and away from the everyday dross. They might as well have been part of the skyline. The moon. The stratosphere. That Wedgwood locket he'd given to her, a simple bauble, a dumb surprise, more precious than a ship of gold.

It was, then, like the paintings, a dreamscape, those eight months. She knew it to the date, never forgot it. December 20 to August 13. The bliss-time of her life. Years later she would look back at that whirling, staggering time. The nights of laughter, running through thunderstorms half-drunk, him on her, next to her, in her, in the alley, laughing, crazy, they were crazy, mad with lust or love or what was it, a longing when the other wasn't there worse than a junkie. She pined for him, a bottomless thirst.

A weekend up at Cape Cod. Seared in her memory. July 3, 1949. The happiest day of her life. Floating around in the water, she on top of him, only three feet of water and floating on his back, pretending to be . . . what? Laughing and splashing— the whole thing—ridiculous! Back then, in her white-and-blue polka-dot bikini, the most stunning girl on the beach, in Cape Cod, on the Eastern shore for God's sake. And he's proud, just fucking proud to be with her.

Edward.

Tall and too thin and from a good family. Edward from Boston who'd seen it all. Edward who was mad about his stop-traffic girl from Odessa. His half-yokel, half–movie star he couldn't stop thinking about, fucking too much, aching for. Oh Lord, let me just spend the rest of my days fucking this girl I love more than I love myself. Which is not much, now that I think about it.

He blindsided her.

When he broke it off. He took his hand and reached into her chest and pulled out everything a girl from Odessa, Texas, can hold.

Why did he do it? How could he have done it? Was it his family? Was it him? Was it someone else? Was it simply being too much in love? Or was he not . . . actually, too much in love? Was he not in love at all? Was she just a fucking fool?

These were the questions that ran through her head, maddening, over and over and over again, kicking her arm out to the nearest glass, throwing her feet out, one in front of the other, to the nearest bar. You see, I'm pretty. You see, I can still stop a room.

And she could, whether at the Downbeat Club or the Onyx or the Three Deuces. She was not less, no, no even more fetching now. There was a sort of melancholy you wanted to shake out of her. A name you wanted to kiss off her lips. And she would go, every night, just as she'd gone before. She didn't give herself one night to mourn he-who-she-would-not-speak-of. Not one night. Dress. Check. Heels. Check. Stockings. Check. Lipstick. Check. Like an army routine. This list, this habit. This was the only thing holding her up. If she hadn't had the checklist, and the bar, and the eight million suitors . . . she would not have made it through.

Still, at the end of the night, alone, having flirted and smiled or even kissed, she would stare in the mirror, those sweetheart lips frozen, that alabaster arm shaking shaking shaking, and watch as that mascara came down in little pieces, droplets, streams. And she would stay frozen, watching her real self, her alone self, what she'd become. After Edward.

And what she'd become was becoming something different, fast. The admirers were still there, yes. Thank God. But inside, the flasks, the shaking. Hidden bottles under the cupboard. Night panics. Her thoughts racing. How easy it would be to break this bottle and take that sharp edge and put it in my neck, my wrists, my gut.

Oh fuck! Fuck this body, fuck this heart. Why?! Why did he do it?

And so, as the nights were getting longer and slurrier and more careless, dangerous, slapdash nights with seedier mornings, it wasn't a difficult decision to make when Lt. Colonel Charles Krause came waltzing through the door of Clark Monroe's Uptown House, went up to the drop-dead girl at the bar, a girl with pitch-black hair and ghost skin, and said, "I'm going to marry you and take you back with me to Michigan."

She laughed at the arrogance. They all did. But looking into his sky-blue eyes and blond crewcut hair, weighing the odds of her ending up with her throat slit on the street against those ice-blue eyes and a place called home with a front porch swing and a man who loved her, she knew. She said to herself, under her lips.

Yes.

FOUR

Danek wasn't about to let anyone leave without realizing he was the smartest kid in the room. The most talented. The one who was going places.

He hadn't thought, driving up to this humble little home, classmates in tow, over the gravel and through the pines, that he would give a flying fuck what these old geezers thought.

Er, he meant, the parents of the victim. Lt. Colonel and Dorothy Krause. I mean, they were ancient. They would probably just blather on the whole time. They would probably smell like soup.

He was prepared. He had a notepad. Different pens. Black with felt tips, for writing faster. He would get what Lars, Brad, and, oh . . . even Katy . . . missed. He, alone, would figure it out. He, alone, would be the hero.

He was not prepared. When the door opened and he saw that face. Jesus. You would not have guessed that Dorothy Krause was in her seventies. I mean, he knew they had children earlier back then, but holy smokes. He thought . . . not thought exactly, maybe felt, when that door opened and that face appeared . . . he felt drawn to walk up the stairs behind her, into the study and stay there, in this house, this home, for the winter.

They were good people.

Yes, it's a simple phrase. One he could hear himself saying in the documentary. He would pause, then, for effect.

Danek Mitchell, what a dreamer!

She had made tea and an assortment of cookies, which they first refused, then picked at, then devoured. Everything placed gracefully on a silver serving tray, a silver service, wasn't that what it was called? You just didn't see it anymore. Tea in a silver serving kettle, on a silver tray, with teacups, tiny dishes beneath, and precious little flowers, daintily flaunting their tricks. Sugar, milk, lemon, if you need it. They just didn't do it like this anymore.

Dorothy Krause. Dotsy. With sable hair, ivory skin, that perfect, damned-near-perfect-placement face and those green, almost emerald eyes.

Simple really, there in a vanilla blouse, gray wool pants. Nothing showy. There were lace embellishments of some sort on the blouse, he couldn't remember, something small and sweet. But her way, her soft, gentle, unassuming way. Her sheer grace. It was disconcerting. Had Beth Krause, yes, Beth Krause, the one they were here about, the one they were gonna win an award with, the one found crumpled by the side of the road, had Beth Krause inherited this grace? These willow eyes? This unassuming, intoxicating nature?

If so, you could see why she was dead.

FIVE

And that could be something, too. The taste of a shell, or the dodge of a hand . . . something always, not infuriatingly, but rivetingly . . . just out of reach.

Danek tried not to think about Dorothy Krause in this way. It was inappropriate. It was ridiculous. And yet.

A sentence never uttered.

A something never had.

He wondered what she carried around underneath that ebony, ink-like crown.

She was a raven.

Odd, wasn't it, that he should feel this, feel anything really, this . . . grappling. And yet, there it was, right in front of him. He wanted to laugh. Wished he could laugh.

He found himself thinking of her, drawn to her name.

Dorothy Krause. What had it been before? Maybe he could ask her. But how could he ask her?

Matter of fact.

Put it with a lot of other questions.

And the name Dorothy. Wasn't that simple? Was she named, after all, after Oz?

Simpletons!

But yet, there she was, Dorothy Krause, with the invisible maiden name. Invisible life. What had she been before she had been . . . his?

His thoughts raced imagining her then, way back then. He did not want to, would not let himself think, count, calculate, how long ago it actually was. He would not add it up.

It dangled right there, right beyond, the edges of what he would and would not think. A thought-not-thought. A word not spoken.

Much like the fleeting glimpse, the don't-allow-yourself-to-think-it image of her daughter draped down dead in the snow. No, no, keep that for someone else to think. Throw it out the back screen door and give it to the sparrows.

No one could hurt her now at least.

SIX

The first week was a bore, unbearable. No snow on the ground, but it was ice-bite, see-your-breath cold. There was no escape. Muskegon, 1952. Trapped there, in the gray, ash landscape, stuck. So far away from the Downbeat Club, the Three Deuces, and Sardi's. She thought she might die. Or, maybe, make herself die, it wasn't that difficult. If she had to, she'd do it. What was all the fuss? And where were all the cocktails? That was the real question.

Weekend excursions, past the still glass lake, Highway 94, over to Chicago. He tried to keep her happy. Nights at Palmer House, fireworks off Navy Pier, games at Wrigley, dinners at the Drake. But, cut to the chase. It was no New York. It was not New York and he was not Edward.

Again, she wondered what had become of him, where had he fallen. Maybe he was still in New York, or maybe Paris, London, knowing him. He could not stay put long. Fancied himself a world traveler. Coming back from Paris, Rome, Venice, he'd put a magnet on his refrigerator, a different magnet, bought on a lark, but a specific lark, from a silly funny gift shop. These Edward would bring home and place lovingly on his fridge in his kicky impress-you apartment on Fifth Avenue. This magnet fridge of trinkets, a cocktail-party conversation piece, a few witticisms in the kitchen, fetching ice. A way of saying, "I've been farther than you. I've been around the world. And I will leave you."

Thinking about those days, weeks, months after he'd slaughtered her in the heart, Dotsy was relieved, grateful to feel nothing. If I can only feel nothing, for the rest of my life, I'll be lucky. Knowing now, thinking it over, what a fool she'd been, a fool for love as they say. Of all the captains of industry, steel magnates, robber-baron sons, war profiteers, of all the bigwigs, postwar moguls and masters of the universe, she'd chosen this one—this losing proposition, this bon vivant, this dilettante. This Edward. If she'd only thought it out, she'd be in a penthouse overlooking the park, not some ranch house in Muskegon, Michigan. But she hadn't thought it out, had she? It had simply run its course.

Even so, she didn't let herself resent her husband. It wasn't Charles's fault. She knew, staring at him rolled silent in his sleep, she knew she was lucky to have him. A good man. Improbable as it was to her, despite her hungover days and nights of spiraling, blitzkrieg intoxication—she'd somehow managed to find a good man. A solid man. A man with his head on his shoulders.

Yes, she knew, in passing, the days he'd spent after the war, before he met her . . . she knew those D-Day stripes and that save-the-world uniform earned him a special reward, a girl reward, and she knew he took it. In spades.

Strange, how that reassured her. Yes, he is bad, too. He can be bad, too. Like me. Dotsy knew she was a hundred percent pure bad person in disguise. It was clear to her. And when Edward gave her the high hat, it was confirmed. Of course he didn't love me,

I'm just a yokel from Odessa, Texas. Loving me would be a humiliation, really. I am a step down. I am a step away from the social register, the Knickerbocker Club, this blue-blood aristocracy and all the things he holds dear.

Still, it cut her in two she'd been so stupid to think it, to fall for him. She should've seen the signs. For instance, what did he "do" exactly? Well, nothing. He was one of the great nothing-doers of New York, a long-held tradition, one to uphold—and he upheld it, martini in hand. What was he really? A dandy. An aesthete. Feckless as the waves lapping the East Egg sound. Christ, she'd never even seen him eat a steak! No, the signs were all there, right from the start, but had she heeded them? No, sir, she'd let herself fall straight in love with this nothing man. This sometime vegetarian. This Hudson scarecrow. This New York "man." A breed grown nowhere else in America. Witty in conversation. Always. Articulate. Check. Well dressed. Well, that goes without saying. On the most polite side of politics but ask him in private, he's quite progressive. Yes, another heartless revolutionary. So kind to those he's never met and cruel to those who loved him.

She hated him.

Disgusted at herself for allowing it to happen. How could she? She was a steadfast girl from Texas, as constant as cactus. She was smarter than that. It's not like she was some lily-lilted girl from Charleston. Some wallflower from Charlotte. The whole thing, as far as she was concerned, was a magic trick.

And then, ten months after she married Charles, came baby. The three months of puking her face off in the toilet, the three months of walking on air, sex fever. The three months of walrus waddling around the house and wanting to say fuck you to the postman. The conked-out birth—she wanted it that way. After nine months of sobriety, she practically grabbed the needle out the doctor's hands and gave the injection herself. Shut it off! Shut off my brain! I'm sick of myself! Waking up in that sterile mint hospital room, Lt. Colonel Charles at her side, a face full of hope, had he been crying? And a so-small tiny baby girl. A gorgeous little pie-face with white hair and saucer blue eyes. A towhead. Elizabeth. My little Beth. We can call her Lizzy or Betsy or Betty. Maybe Betsy. Betsy and Dotsy. My little own baby girl. A drug made of love coursing through her brain, her heart, her veins.

No, after that, she couldn't have picked out Edward from a lineup of Franco, Mussolini, and Hitler. He had disappeared, somehow. The space in her memory taken up, knocked out, bulled over for new space. Baby space. Love-for-baby-girl space. And now Edward was nothing more than a question mark. Who? Oh . . . him . . . right. Yes. I remember. Kind of.

Like an early child memory before three, there it goes. Gone for good. And suddenly it was like it had never happened. Not cured, exactly. Just never was. Erased.

But, she'd heard something, something not entirely insubstantial, from her girlfriends back at Sardi's. He'd not come to much. He'd never managed to get the airplane off the ground, so to speak. They said, to her disguised delight, "He's gotten older. You wouldn't recognize him, Dots."

And Dotsy would pretend this was never-care news, weather news, sports-team news. "And the other thing, Dots. You'll never believe it. He's asked about you. All the girls . . . Ethel, Irene, Rita, too. In whispers, late night. Asked about you and your husband. How could you leave?"

Dotsy stiffing up now, baby cooing up from her basket, little basket on the table, swaddled in pink. A love bug. A snug little bean. "Dotsy, he gets shit-faced and asks about you. I swear. You wouldn't recognize him. He's lost it. Whatever it was, I swear, he lost it."

And Dorothy Krause wishing she were the kind of person who could transcend idle gossip, wishing she were the angel-face she knew she was supposed to be, couldn't help, upon putting down the receiver, *click*, looking down at her pink baby towhead swaddled and big-eyed and pudgy, couldn't help but think, a self-ish little greedy greedy thought, a thought she shouldn't allow herself, a slaying thought.

Ha. I won.

SEVEN

How stupid they found themselves. Disgusting. Thinking about those moments before they had met the Krauses, or then . . . the victim's parents. It had meant nothing to them. Names on a paper, nothing more.

And now, they couldn't bear to look at each other. Never mentioned it, not even in passing. Danek at Katy, Brad at Lars, Lars at Danek. Knowing that six months earlier they had actually contrived . . . a trap. A trap for the Krauses! They would make them cry on camera! Now that would make the documentary.

But that was before.

And now . . . half a year later, sitting in the unassuming, well-appointed blue, a sitting room neat as a pleat, across from Lt. Colonel Charles and his fair wife, Dorothy . . . they might as well have stapled their belly buttons to their spines. Rot gut. A blushing guilt.

There she was, offering cookies or tea or maybe a sandwich. There he was, the crewcut haircut now gray, the black-and-white soldier photographs framed behind resting on the nook. The blue-and-green curtains, the doilies on the side table, spick-and-span, the sepia wedding photograph on the mantel, the kind words . . .

No, there would be no crying today. In fact, there would be no crying at all. No dramatics.

They were not dramatic people, the Krauses. No, the opposite. There was an effortless grace. In her ivory sweater set and onyx hair . . . there was a quiet resilience that condemned even as it enthralled.

They would not break down. There would be no Jerry Springer moment, no taking out their baby's old tokens and weeping, no references to "before the accident."

They were matter-of-fact. They were transcendent. They were everything that Danek, Lars, Brad, and Katy were not. They were the old time. The old way. The Greatest Generation.

It wasn't until leaving, after the third afternoon of filming, walking down the walkway, gliding past the white picket fence and into the horrible now, that Danek had ever truly realized the meaning of the expression.

The Greatest Generation.

(There will never be another.)

It was a drive due east, past the Hampton Inn, to get to Shauna. It was a drive where there were a million things to say but better not say them. Brad mentioned something about the Packers, met with a dull nod.

They had known they were young but they had not known they were foolish. Until now. They would not forget it. They would make it up to the Krauses. This imaginary crime. They had wanted to take advantage of them. Yes, it was before they knew them. Yes. But that had been their motive. To make them cry. To stir up drama. To get a good grade. The thought now, a lump in the throat.

Pulling up to the curb, the apartment complex, apologizing from the pavement.

And inside . . . look here, Shauna Boggs.

There she sits, must be sitting anyway, in the living room slash dining room slash . . . bedroom? What exactly is this place? This crappy little shit-hole in the middle of town yet not here. You would walk past it and never know it was here. Seeing it and not seeing it at the same time. A bland oasis.

Beige, what is it, stucco? Or a form of stucco? Faux stucco? An apartment complex built in the '70s, maybe late '60s. Tame as a Twinkie.

And there she sits, three-hundred-pound Shauna Boggs with her not-blonde, not-brown hair, somehow greasy at the scalp and dry at the ends. A cautionary tale in split ends.

She is wearing a sweatshirt. With a dog on it. The dog stares plaintively from her gloppy, overflowing chest. Below that, jeans, stretch jeans with an elastic waist. Shmoo jeans. Shmoo sweatshirt. Shmoo look. Her skin, a lightless sort of beige. A paste. Her eyes, swallowed by her cheeks. Her mouth, thin and dry and blending backward into her face.

From her: dramatics.

As difficult as it was, the students, to see themselves, to be themselves, at the Lt. Colonel's house, here they were like kings. Although she didn't offer them anything. More like she sat and waited, waited for what . . . them to like her? Them to accept her. Them to tell her she was there.

How could they turn off the camera when . . . when behind her there is a sink full of dishes, sideways on a slant, and at her feet is a cat toy and she has the kitty litter right under the table. No, it was too good. Keep the camera running. Let's get this.

And the tears. The blubbering. Slobby, sniveling tears into the Kleenex and the snot, too. A lesson in Americanism. Now. Hysterics. Drama in a stucco complex. Sadness the depth of a cereal box.

So, there she is, for all to see, forever, sobbing into the camera, saying, "I just . . . I just can't understand who would do such a thing. . . . And how . . . even now . . . after all these years . . . they could live with themselves." Snivel. Blow nose. Blot face.

"I know I couldn't."

EIGHT

The motel clerk who'd hired Beth all those centuries ago had a taut stretched face from smoking and stretching and smoking and stretching her skin. Pull pull pulling it tight tight and over her ears, sewing it, bolting it down. It seems she'd hit it big, this banana-haired lady, married an auto exec, moved to Bloomfield Hills. Those coupon days back in Muskegon, a thing of never-talking, a thing of leave-behind.

Here, at the Radisson Lobby Bar in Bloomfield Hills, you would not believe she had been the one to actually hire Beth. But Danek and Katy had driven out here, three hours, to get it right.

It wasn't drinking time but black roots was having a drink. The white wine spritzer set down before her at the lobby bar, guilty, on the tiny circle table, had prompted her.

"It's five o'clock somewhere."

Danek and Katy had smiled politely, not wanting to seem snooty, wanting to take off this college kid armor, leave it at coatcheck, don it later. Now we are investigators. Now we are friends.

Danek had typed up the list of questions. Katy would ask them, of course, she'd be better. Put the lady at ease. Girl talk.

"Do you remember the afternoon you hired Beth Krause? At the Green Mill Inn?"

"Barely. Honestly, look. It's been awhile."

Staring nervously into the camera. How do I look? Fluffing up her hair. Danek behind the camera . . . fine . . . you look fine. Great even. Don't change a thing. Just try to focus on the questions. Try to remember.

"Even just a small thing?"

"Well, I . . . I remember she seemed kind of out of place, you know? She seemed kind of like . . . well, I was thinking, What do you want this shit-ass job for? A pretty girl like you."

Katy laughed with her, a casual we're-in-it-together laugh. Keep her happy. Keep her comfortable.

"I guess I worked there, so why not, right? I wasn't that bad to look at. Not then anyway."

"Oh, c'mon, you look great, are you kidding?"

Keep her cozy. All is well.

She shrugs now, "A shitty job's a shitty job, you know. No matter how you slice it."

"That is for sure. I've had my fair share."

A lie, of course. Katy had never had a job, other than babysitting her cousin over summers in Saginaw. A family job. A job to say you've had a job. Teach the value of a dollar. But not really. Not a crapsicle french fry job, not a frazzle-brain, answer-twelve-phone-lines front desk job. A kid job, no danger of an accidental brush with humanity. That cement block future of toil.

"You have?" Blondie looks relieved. We're peers. "Oh good. Well, that's what this was."

"And what did it entail?"

Danek behind the camera, Danek thinking about ordering a drink. Maybe a gin and tonic. Maybe a Pimm's. No, too summery. Maybe a whiskey and Coke. Maybe one for Katy, too. That might work.

"You know, we had to check people in, check 'em out. Simple stuff."

The tiny circle table gets emptied. A replacement drink gets set down. No questions asked. Guess she's a regular.

"Was there ever any weird people coming through? When you were there? Anyone you'd suspect?"

Slurp. Clink.

"Well, you know, we had some odd ones, yes. But mostly it was the groups I hated. We had a few Hells Angels. Real rowdy, you know?"

"Hells Angels?"

"Oh yeah. Biker guys. All in leather. And some union guys. Sometimes there'd be some hubbub down at the plants . . . next thing you know we'd be checking in the union guys."

"What about a lone individual? Did you ever check in someone you thought, 'Oh no, hide my purse!'"

Katy smiles. Reach out to them. Make them feel like you are gonna be best friends for sure.

"Look, there were some creeps. I'm not gonna lie. One guy even offered me five hundred bucks to go up to his room. Just to watch him . . . you know. A real normal-looking guy, too. I'm not kidding."

"Really?"

"Oh, yeah. And there was this one guy asked if I would . . . uh, forget it."

"No, c'mon, I have to know now."

"Okay, well, there was this one guy, wanted me to come up and call him names, like call him a baby, and he'd put on diapers and shake a rattle and stuff. Offered me three hundred dollars. Said that was it . . . that was all I had to do."

"Wow. Did you do it?"

"Hell, no! I mean, sure, sounds like easy money but . . . you never know."

"Unbelievable."

"I know! But, you know, it was mostly people traveling through, families on a budget, you know. In summers, lots of fishing. Peak season. The rest of the year, well, we had some husbands, getting their rocks off, on the side. They'd pay for the night, be gone by twelve."

"But no one in particular, maybe a regular?"

"Not really. Creeps are creeps, you know."

A giant diamond ring on her finger, single setting on a spray-tan hand. Must be at least ten grand. Right there, in sparkles. Ice on her hand, ice in the glass. *Clink clink clink.*

"And Beth? Do you remember anything particular about her? Anything odd that mighta stuck."

"Well, I don't know. Maybe I shouldn't say but . . . she seemed. . . . It was weird. I felt like, she seemed frail somehow. Like, she couldn't remember anything, you know. She couldn't even remember her own name."

Slurp. Swivel the ice.

"I remember thinking . . . this poor kid. Man, she has no idea." *Clink.*

"I mean, she is in for it."

NINE

Shot in his arm, one shot in his side, he'd been lucky. No vital organs. Just barely. The randomness of fate, a broken weather vane, careening in the wind.

Nineteen forty-four. A practical joke, waking up in this whispery, bleached, spick-and-span place after the *ratatat-tat, ratatat-tat* of that killing shore at Omaha Beach. Muck and water and spiderweb blood, dodging bullets in the brine, a kind of chaos worse than death itself. And yet, death all around, practically promenading down the beach in a black robe and parasol, "Yes, yes, children. Keep it up. Bring me more. More! You are prolific today. A great day. A hallowed day. A banner day for death."

And then this here, this hall of alabaster, almost a church in its respectful, stone silence. Waking up the first time, for seconds only, above him a nurse and doctor in matching white coats and matching white concerned postures.

"And how is our patient?"

"Lt. Colonel? Lt. Colonel Krause? Can you hear me? Can you hear my voice?"

And briefly, the thought "Have I made it to heaven? Is this the immaculate fluffy cloud place I've been hearing so much about? If so, I'd thought the nurses would be better looking." And then a laugh, to himself.

A laugh coming out of the patient.

"He's delirious."

"He'll be fine. Keep an eye on him."

And the sound of the matching white coats moving away, moving away now to another sucker lying on his back, mummified. Resentful, betrayed somehow, to hear, "Private Reiter. Can you hear me? Can you hear my voice?"

Same shtick. Same shtick, different sucker.

And then the blanket of sleep, a gauze of days, hours, weeks spent flat-back hearing the whispers echoing off the walls, from far away an occasional scream, a few times, late night, the sound of a grown man crying. Muddled sobs in the moonlight, muttering retreats, buried in the pillow. Shh.

The second time waking, more substantial, a stronger visit.

"Can you hear me? Can you hear my voice?"

Eyes blinking, a different nurse. This one, a brunette with a face like a pie, a sweetheart face. Maybe this is heaven. Ah, is there anything better than bleeding out on a death-walk tide and waking up to a pie-face cherub of a girl in a cotton starch hat? A system contrived to melt your heart into goop. For you, I'll do anything. You saved me. You saved me from that death-waltz shore.

Stirring, trying to get up. "Where am I? Where is this?"

"Don't get up, please, Lt. Colonel. There. That's better. This is Charterhouse Military Hospital. Recovery Ward."

The name a homing device, a passkey, a map.

"You're healing. That's your job now. Getting strong again. Let's don't rush it."

The brunette hair a shade darker than mouse but lighter than chestnut. An English kind of hair, no dyes. An English face, no button nose, but a funny shape anyway. A drastic shape, cut off too early.

"What's your name, nurse? I want to tell my friends back home about the pretty nurses they have over here."

"Oh, now." Straightening his pillow above his head, leaning forward, placing his blanket just so.

"Lucy. My name's Lucy."

"Well, then. I'll tell the folks back in the States that the best-looking Lucys come from England. It's the only place for Lucys."

"Oh, come now. You rest."

And then, back into the painkiller gauze, back into the cobweb dreams in a place made of stone, chalk sheets, and 3 AM sobbing.

Getting out a month later, he seemed taken over by a death drive, a gulping, grabbing, smoking endless void to fill with only one thing. Girls.

Girls were the answer to that stretch of grim reaper sand and that *ratatat-tat* he heard nightly, sometimes waking him from sleep. Blonde girls. Brown girls. Redheaded girls. Tall girls. Short girls. Girls with nothing to 'em. Girls with big tits and red-painted lips. Girls with black hair. Girls with platinum blonde hair. Girls with honey-colored Rita Hayworth tresses in tight-fitting sweaters and peach silk dresses.

There was no amount of girls to quench this death thirst, not that he didn't try. Oh, did he ever. Sometimes two girls in one night. One for dinner. One for drinks. It was easy, in that save-the-world uniform, with that save-the-day story, the troops spreading out over France, pushing the bastard Krauts back. And Patton, well, you gotta love the guy, one thing about that reckless son of a bitch, he knew how to win a war, that's for sure. Trouncing the Germans, trampling them into the fields, outsmarting those sneaky fuckers. We'll show you how it's done. Bastards.

And the reports, coming back from the front, horror-eyed clips about stick figures in stripes, camps of bodies, ovens. Ovens! It was inconceivable. It couldn't be true. Could it? Everyone asking everyone, have you heard, have you heard? Sick fucks. Good thing we have Patton.

Girls cure it! Girls make it go away. Late night or early night or any time of day, really. Drawn-on pantyhose, don't have to draw them off. A parade of buckles and hooks and clasps, blood-red lipstick, hot roller curls, cascading down, transparent bready flesh and below, somehow, the shuddering forgetting of the *ratatat-tat*. Mary, Ethel, Rita, Rose, Lizzie, Catherine, Betty, Angie, Kate, Amelia, Amanda, Abigail, Mabel, Isabel, Izzy, Grace. All of them, all of them colliding into one flickering late-night clamoring bliss. And then, the next day, another.

Shipping back to the States, back home to Muskegon, recovered, he'd stop over in New York, just for a few days, to celebrate. Knowing, too, that in New York, there would be more of this, more girl frenzy, more girl medicine.

And walking into Clark Monroe's Uptown House, he had every intention of a blonde, brunette, redheaded girl marathon, until he saw across the bar a raven-haired girl who didn't give a fuck about him.

A girl named Dotsy.

TEN

Whooping cough. Pertussis. Three months old. Twelve weeks in this world and there they were, racing through each light, red lights even, to get to Mercy General Hospital before paroxysm, seizure, death.

Elizabeth Lynn Krause, an infant, not gonna make it. That's not what they said, but you could tell, that's what they were thinking. A newborn nose crusted over in snot, that *flek flek flek, hoop hoop hoop*, over and over.

The nurse had practically grabbed the baby and thrown her in the Mercy General ER herself. Tubes and pipes, pipes and tubes, a pipe in her mouth, to clear the lungs, a tube down her throat. Breathe, baby, breathe. Lord above, clear out this gunk, do not slaughter this innocent.

And Dotsy, after all she'd been though. The nine months of waddling, the conked-out childbirth, the breast to baby's lips.

The truth of the matter is, before the nine months, Dotsy'd always been what they liked to call "nervous." Frantic. Terrified. Misfiring. A brain full of turning gears and pistons, backfiring, broken, sped up somehow. Her brain a constant tumbling, a careening landscape, a frenzied paralysis of fear, terror, hysteria, pointed, sparked by . . . nothing. A panic dread. A blank canvas urgency to do . . . what?

That was what the drink was for. The stiff cocktail was to quell the panic. Calm down! Stay still! Stop spinning! It was only the firewater remedy that put this riveting panic brain to rest. Shut it off. Please someone put a wrench in the gears. And the vodka was the wrench. And the gin. And the whiskey. For others, a pleasure. For her, medicine. Panic killer. Brain freeze.

But the nine months had shifted the startle gears, too, somehow. The pulsing, rushed, stubborn hormones had taken over Dotsy and set her down to rest each night. You're okay. You're okay now. Sleep.

The storm had subsided. Nine months of serene, tranquil waters. Yes, she knew it was the hormones, of course. But knowing didn't break the spell. Basal nature. Stubborn, willful, unrelenting.

And when the baby arrived, the breast to her mouth, the neurotransmitters, hormones, had flooded the waters again. Oxytocin. Love drug. Love your baby. You will never stop. You will protect this crying, goopy thing with your life. You never knew, did you? Well, Dotsy, this is it.

And the nursing, again, a drug of calm, serenity, tide. A body drug of peace, an armor of ardor. A shield. You are happy. You are happy now. All is passed. Everything is as it should be.

And Dotsy knowing, knowing it was a trick, an ambush, releasing halcyon into the blood. But again, knowing was irrelevant, superfluous, laughable even. Knowing didn't change it. Unrelenting nature. Miracle bodies.

And how Dotsy had hated her body, too, all those years before. What is this thing? What is this thing I have to go around in? What is this thing bleeding and bubbling and burbling? This secret thing, I can't tell anyone. She hated this thing. Didn't everyone? Wasn't that the point of being a girl? To hate this flesh that bleeds, this bread body, this too-vulnerable carousel, this danger-part below. This place where they'll get you.

A body of secrets and shames and holes. A panic body. A fear vessel. A hurt-me cast.

But the nine months of calm drug, the three hours of love drug, well . . . suddenly the body was not any of these shames and holes and embarrassments. The body was a fucking miracle. How did it do that? Where did that milk come from? How did it know to keep going? How did it know to change when the baby changed? Grow when the baby grew? Give the baby just what it needed, when it needed it? The right milk, the right chemistry? Each day, each week, each month, every month, after baby was born? Grow with baby? Change with baby? Shut off when baby was done? Only enough for baby? Unattainable, a mystery still, for science. All those lab technicians in white coats cannot do what one breast does without thinking.

Ha!

Why did I hate this thing again? The "weaker" sex. The "rotten walls." The "feminine" vessel. Ha! What a laugh. Thinking, more than once, a joke but not a joke . . . if men had babies we'd be extinct. Dotsy went from frantic panic lush to calm love drug cherub without transition. Without awareness. Without strife. An accidental transformation. But a saving one. Nevertheless.

And then, with little Elizabeth baby girl *whoop whooping* in Mercy General Hospital, in the ER, poked and prodded with tubes and pipes . . . Dotsy knew, knew in every cell of her veins . . . if the baby goes, I go, too. Where the baby ends, I end, too.

Bury me with her. Bury me under the ground and I will hold her through eternity. I will wrap myself around her and kick off fate, protect her through the tides and the rapture and the infinite beyond. I will slip down deep under the dirt and carry her home.

You cannot take her away from me. You cannot bury my baby. Bury me, oh Lord. Bury me.

The panic of not knowing, the panic of not being able to fix it, the panic of helplessness. Fear. Worry. Screaming, pulverizing terror. Those days in August 1956. Those not-know days. Those stab-your-heart days. Dotsy spent mornings in Mercy General Emergency. Nights in Mercy General Ward. The Lt. Colonel begging her to come home. Sleep. You must rest. Please.

Sleep!

As if it were possible. No sleep. I'll sleep when she sleeps. I'll sleep when she sleeps forever. You won't be able to wake me up then. Just try.

And that final night, the end night, the night they all knew she was going, it was over.

Dotsy had ducked out, around the block to a place called Dreamers, a far cry from the Downbeat Club on 52nd. A shit-basket watering hole full of bloats. An end-your-life hole. A give-up.

In this place, knowing she would have to end her life tomorrow, tear her skin off, what would she do, how would she do it, knowing she would have to burrow down into the boot hill dirt, the cemetery bed. Dotsy had proceeded to get shit-faced.

The panic button pushed, the terror gears grinding, the dizzying abyss had, after nine months of bliss and then three, caught up with her. Here it was again, say a greeting now to your old friend panic. Your lifelong friend. The one you trust. You thought you'd gotten away, didn't you? With that nine months, and that baby girl, and that magic body, chest of gold? You'd thought it was over, this spinning cycle of fear? Well, drink up, Dotsy. It's gonna be a long life.

"I'll have another."

Gulp.

"I'll have another."

Throw it back.

"I'll have another."

'Til the stool starts somehow not to hold and the mirror-glass wall of bottles starts to spin like a merry-go-round and suddenly, blissfully, thankfully, the panic-head flies up and Dorothy Krause, the Lt. Colonel's wife, sways woozy off the bar stool onto the floor. The white-and-black checker tiles get to spin, too, and suddenly all the world is a white-and-black tornado and there are voices, yes, there are—but they are far away, up and above this spinning carnival ride, another ride, another promenade.

And the Lt. Colonel gets called, out, out of his dreams in the middle of 2 AM. And there she is, his handsome wife from Odessa, lying broken on the white-and-black tile of this crap-lounge called Dreamers.

A husband gets to walk through the pore-blotch faces, the bloodshot eyes, the flannels. A husband gets to pick up his wife off the floor and carry her, with the bartender, back to the car, back to the house. Back to the bed. A husband gets to take off her shoes. One shoe. Two shoe. Red skirt. Blue shoe. A husband gets to lie his wife on the bedspread and place her, tuck her tight. Quiet. Gentle. Silent. A husband gets to love his wife, helpless. To want to tear out his heart and give it to her. Replace her broken pieces. Take me. Take me, Dotsy. I will deliver you.

And, in the morning, the kitchen dawn of the day, the coffee grinds brewing in the kitchen, the phone rings and the phone gets picked up and there's a pause, a miracle pause, a savior pause. And the Lt. Colonel puts down the receiver and stares at the ceiling. A husband gets to tell his wife.

"She made it. Our baby girl made it."

A wife gets to cry into her pillow, thank you. A wife gets to whisper thank you, Lord. A wife gets to hold her baby again and never, ever let her go.

A wife gets to stand there, forty-seven years later, in the middle of Beth's room. Light blue. The white wood doll bed and dresser, the white gilded mirror, the light blue curtains, the white closet door, a wife gets to stare at a portrait while, somewhere in town, a projector flickers round and round, telling how her baby girl got put six feet in the ground.

ELEVEN

The facts.

On March 3, 1978, Elizabeth Lynn Krause, age twenty-two, clocked in at 6 PM for an eight-hour shift at the Green Mill Inn.

There was snow on the ground. It was a brisk thirteen degrees, with a seven-below wind chill.

At 9:15, an anonymous 911 phone call was made. "Please . . . something's wrong . . . there's noises . . . a robbery." A man's voice, middle-aged.

Two days later, Beth Krause was found on the outskirts of town, off Route 31, dumped by a tree, in ripped clothes with multiple injuries, pummeled, strangled, and discarded. Around her neck, a Wedgwood locket, blue and white.

These were the same facts from years ago. Nothing new. So it was strange that now, twenty-five years later, Detective Samuel Barnett, now a thirty-year veteran of the Muskegon Police Force, would look up at that screen, that small-town screen playing that small-town documentary, and say to himself quite simply, in the parlance of the town, "Something's jacked."

But that's exactly what he did.

As the students, sweet kids, Lars, Danek, Brad, and Katy were congratulated lavishly by the townsfolk, fellow students, and even fellow members of the force . . . although "force" was a strong word for the boys in blue from Muskegon. They were more of an "inkling." As Lt. Colonel Charles Krause and his elegant wife, Dorothy, were noticeably absent, but thanked nevertheless, Detective Barnett had his mind on a clock.

Yes, it was the clock that ticked and tocked and beat its hideous heart between his ears, chiming its way through his cranium and emerging front and center, as elegant as an atom.

The clock said 8:45.

Don't you see? The clock, thrown willy-nilly next to that crappy little safe in that crappy little wood-paneled office of the Green Mill Inn, said 8:45.

But the robbery . . . according to the 911 phone call, was taking place at 9:15.

All this time it had been thought, the innocent bystander on the 911 call had said, "There's been a robbery." Past tense. But no. The tape was played and replayed in the film. The commotion, the "something wrong" was supposedly happening at 9:15. But the clock, in the background of the crime scene, frozen now forever on celluloid, was stopped at 8:45.

He could kick himself for missing it. Yes, he was a rookie, but goddammit.

Through the muttering, smattering of minions, Detective Samuel Barnett wedged his way, whispering in the ear of poor little rich Danek, frightened by the urgency of the cop.

"Play it again."

"Excuse me." Danek wondered if this was some strange form of compliment. Not a request.

"Play it again."

Silence.

"But, sir—"

"Listen, kid, all I'm asking is you close those doors, grab the projectionist, and play it again."

"Right now?"

Danek didn't know if he was angry or thrilled. What should he be? He was both.

"Yes, kid, right now."

And that was that, cops get their way in little podunk towns, especially with college students with straight A's and aspirations toward, what, the Supreme Court, the attorney general, the presidency.

Yes, of course, Danek would replay the documentary . . . a private screening for the detective. How thrilling! Flattering, really.

Let the flicker down, draw the curtain up, make the small room a place of thinking. Danek wondered if this would help him get into Princeton.

PART III

Maybe it was excessive to go over there so much, the day after Thanksgiving, the day before Christmas, to set up the tree, take out the ornaments, boxes from storage, to buy the Douglas fir, to fix the tiny white glitter lights, to string the tinsel, to hang the stockings, and to do so all to a selection, sappy indeed, of Christmas music, carols, chosen by Danek, of course, on this newfangled thing, this iPod, he had exhibited to a chorus of *oohs* and *aahs*.

But, somehow, in the first Michigan snows of winter, that last gasp of 2003, it had become obvious to Lars, Danek, Brad, and Katy that the two silver-age people at 2226 Rose Avenue would not be left alone for the holidays but should, from this point forward, be showered with an embarrassment of attention and activity and animation through the arch of holidays from Thanksgiving to Christmas to New Year's. Or maybe it was a sense of family, lost, to each of them, family far, far away and somehow estranged.

Or maybe it was the guilt. A collective guilt, never uttered.

They would make it up. They were good kids.

They would fix it.

To meet there, the four of them, Danek with his carols, Katy with those glass-spun ornaments, Lars and Brad with the Douglas fir tree, tinsel, and even a poinsettia bought almost out of the gate of that tree farm down on Flint Ridge, to usher in this new season with a new sense of sentiment, a protective sense of sheltering . . . well, yes, it was new to them. It was new to them all, a unanimous surprise matched, held, trumped by the opening of doors to that spick-and-span ocean-blue living room, a fire, and the smells of pecan pie, pumpkin pie, turkey, gravy, stuffing, mashed potatoes, sweet potatoes, and booze, too, a winter kind of brown booze, poured mischievously into eggnog with sprinkles and cloves and a wink, just this once.

In the background, the Packers game, and the house a buzz of activity, who can help who, what can I do to help, can I get that, here let me hold that for you, falling over one another to help, falling into one another, a frenzy of cinnamon and pecans and pinecones and a thousand gestures, going outward, away from you, what can I give? Let me give more. Let me do more. What can I give?

And strange to them all, Lars, Danek, Brad, and Katy, that somehow this toast, on this day, so many miles away from Mom and Dad and aunts and uncles back home, this time around the table, with the red winter tablecloth in that sky-blue room, somehow meant more, somehow held more, a cling to the heart, an absolution, a deliverance even. A new angel on the tippy-top of the tree, passing yams and chatter at that ruby-set table with the Lt. Colonel and his onyx-haired Dotsy, Packers in the background, 10–7.

So, it was strange then, too, when, in the middle of just-before dessert, a knock comes to the door and outside, then, is none other than the blob, Shauna Boggs, in her cowl-neck and parka, a shimmering turtle veering outside the door frame, leaning slightly to the left.

TWO

An aisle among many aisles at the Walmart. Big and blue and full of stuff. So much stuff! Stuff for your kitchen. Stuff for your playroom. Stuff for your bedroom. Stuff for your bath. Garden stuff. Lawn stuff. Baby stuff. Car stuff. Stereo stuff. Kid stuff. Dad stuff. Stuff for stuff. Stuff to store your stuff. Enough stuff to put your other stuff to shame. So much stuff. Never enough stuff. Never enough stuff to fix the stuff you can't ever, ever fix with stuff.

And for Shauna, in the aisles and aisles of stuff, an idea. I know! I know what I will do! Wading through the miles and miles of aisles and aisles, there is a jewelry area. Jewelry. And there is a plate area. Maybe plates? And, finally, an area of crystal ware. Crystal. Yes, crystal. Glasses, candlesticks, a vase for a bouquet. A classy vase, a vase with roses etched on the side. Then I'll put roses in it, roses in roses, get it?

And, also, on the way out, Shauna catches it out of the corner of her eye. Peppermint schnapps. Peppermint schnapps, now that's festive.

I will come bearing gifts, a rose vase with roses and peppermint schnapps. You can mix it with cocoa. Isn't that what you do?

Mix it with hot cocoa and sip it by the fire. Just like a family. Like a family we will sit in that ice-blue living room and sip schnapps-spiked cocoa by the fire.

I'll buy cocoa, too. They probably have it but I'll buy it anyway. Better safe than sorry.

It had bothered her. The kids. Coming to her door. What had it meant? What could it mean? That photograph of Beth. That article. Why had they brought it? She was my friend, not theirs. I know damn well what she looks like, you don't think I know? Jesus.

But Dorothy and the Lt. Colonel, they won't be expecting me. Of course they won't. But, bearing gifts, I mean, what's the worst they can do? No, no. They will welcome me. They will welcome me, probably no one there, probably they're just sitting around, watching football, it's Sunday, yes, he'll be watching the Packers. Dotsy will be making sauerbraten and the Lt. Colonel will be sitting in his chair yelling and praising, praising and yelling at Brett Favre. Hell, the fire will already be going. They are bound to invite me in, why wouldn't they?

Standing at the checkout line, Shauna Boggs notices the young, too-pretty girl, all in makeup behind her bright blue smock and ROLL-IT-BACK pin. The little bitch is making her nose smaller and averting her gaze. What? You're too good for me? You think you're better than me? Oh, I get it. I'm just some fat slob. Just some fat ugly old cow to you, is that right? Little cunt, I could show you. Little cunty cunt. I'll get you. I'll get you and your little dog, too.

Give me that bag! Give me that receipt. Fuck. You'd think I was a goddamned leper. Jesus. I bought my parka here for God's sake. How's that for gratitude? This great big Walmart, this big blue betrayal, you were meant to embrace me.

In the parking lot, lit from above in patches from high-above steel lampposts, sentinels in the concrete, guarding the lot while the sun falls down under the dirt-gray sky and now come little flutters, little flutters of frost. Down in the slow fall, a descent of purpose, as inevitable as night itself dipping down, conquering slowly in white. Here we are, here we come to grace you, to cover you in white. Sleep, sleep now, it's over. The champagne-colored Nissan is hard to find at first, it's not the only one and the lot is crowded. God, Christmas. Fuck Christmas.

This goddamn rush every year, this frenzy. You'd think it was the first time, each time, for fuck's sake. And, I know it's not me, it's getting worse each year. I just know it is. Each year, earlier and more frenzied. It didn't used to be like this. Used to be, things were delicate. Small and special. Quieter. Used to be there wasn't even this parking lot. Or this goddamned Walmart. Used to be, there was a little strip downtown, they'd light it up. Remember that? They'd light it up after Thanksgiving, and put a tree, and put some lights up in rows, with tinsel, twenty feet apart. A colonnade down Main Street. A promenade and we would walk it. We would walk through it, me and Beth, we'd walk along giggling into our mittens, snowflakes clinging to our scarves, and there'd be dumb little carols, "Let's hear those sleigh bells jingling, ring-ting-tingling, too, come on it's lovely weather for a sleigh ride together with you." "Si-iilent night. Hoo-ooly night. Aaa-all is calm. Aaa-all is bright . . . "

And we'd cuss and curse the dumb-ass carols, saying how

we were gonna smash the speakers hanging down from the lights, pull the plug. Beth in her baby-blue wool hat and scarf.

Those black suede boots, remember them? They went up to just below the knee and even a stacked black heel. Classy. But, you know, that'll be the day.

And Beth said she just had to have a hot dog and left me there in front of the Walgreens, snow coming down. I was pissed. I remember, cursing to myself, I almost left. Coulda just left you there, little miss perfect. And then, feeling so stupid, what a jerk-face, when next week I open that bright red rectangle mystery present back home and it's the that'll-be-the-day boots, right there in front of me, black suede boots, stacked heel, with a note:

"From Santa Claus aka Beth. HA-HA, you thought I left you for a hot dog!"

And I could've fallen off the face of the earth backward.

Yes. 1976. Things were different.

Their friendship, a castle made of sand. That day on the playground, years before. Beth, not even five years old, building a castle, all to herself. Four turrets and a tower. Even a moat. Around her, the older boys circling, running, shouting, playing pirate, playing spaceship, playing cowboys and Indians. In between them, Beth, the eye of the storm, meticulous, building, shaving, sculpting. And Shauna, one of the boys. Trying to be, anyway. But even then, outcast. They all knew where she lived. That dare-you-to-go-in house.

One of the boys, the freckle-faced one, had taken an especially diabolical pleasure in destroying the castle, devastated in one kick. And Beth, seeing the four turrets and the tower and the moat, annihilated, burst into tears. It was Shauna, then, who saved the day. Shauna, then, who came to her defense, who walked right up to the freckle-faced boy and punched him. Punched him! Right in the nose.

Then chaos on the playground. The boy's nose streaming out blood, the little girls screaming, running to their mommies, and Beth looking up as if watching a play. Shauna had grabbed her by the hand and whisked her out of there.

"C'mon, I know where to hide!"

And they had sprinted, the scene falling back behind them. A gaggle of moms looking for the culprit. Of course it couldn't have been a girl. Climbing up up up into a century-old elm at the other side of the park, peeking in. They couldn't help but giggle. They were criminals. They were partners in crime. They were in love in that moment. And that moment lasted for years.

It was only later, when Beth got into Hope and Shauna got into no hope, that the castle made of sand began to disintegrate. Weakened now. Exposed. Vulnerable to any kick on the playground from an errant boy.

Yes. Those schoolgirl days. Things were different.

Shauna now, thinking, this peppermint schnapps might not be right for a gift. Maybe it's disrespectful, even. What if they think I'm saying something bad, like, "Here. Here's a drink. I bet you could use it."

No, no, this peppermint schnapps is not a good idea. It cheapens it. Cheapens the vase with the tiny scratch roses and red roses, too. That's enough. That'll do. It's a classy gift. Thought out.

Better just leave the schnapps out of it. Better just keep that to myself. Can't bring it back anyway, no way, not to missus cunty cunt back there. The look she'd give me. Little bitch.

No, best to keep the schnapps out of it. Best to drink it. Maybe just a sip. Dutch courage.

THREE

The kitchen is a place you take someone when you're not sure you want them to stay. And so it was that Shauna Boggs found herself standing in the middle of the holiday-scent kitchen, surrounded by Danek, Lars, Brad, Katy, and, of course, Dorothy Krause, too. The Lt. Colonel, in the other room, had said a perfunctory salutation, a nod of acknowledgment, but it was fourth quarter, what could he do? Danek was treating this like a scene from a TV drama, he had seen this setup before, he would have to learn these skills, one day, as a senator. The unwelcome guest. The unhappy constituent. It was all practice, everything was practice for those years on the Hill.

"Shauna, please, would you like something? Some water, maybe some coffee?"

But Shauna doesn't hear him, or see him, or acknowledge him. Shauna is too busy proffering her big silver-and-gold present, something in a festive shiny paper bag, with sparkles and fleur-de-lis tissue paper. Something heavy, she hands it to Dotsy, solemn, "Merry Christmas, Mrs. Krause."

And now, still in her parka, no one has asked her to take it off, Dorothy takes the silver-and-gold regency bag. "Oh, Shauna. That was so sweet of you. How kind. You didn't have to."

And Shauna, wondering now, why haven't they asked me to sit down? Why haven't they asked me to take off my coat? Why are we not all sat down around the fire sipping cocoa? Why am I not welcome here?

Why are these kids here? These four dumb, smug, Gap catalog kids? Why are they looking at me like a problem to be solved? Something to be dealt with? Why the formality? Oh, yes, Shauna. Shauna, would you like some coffee? What's with all the coffee? Is there a fucking exam in the morning? Geesh.

Well, no matter. Dots will open the present and all will be forgiven. Good old Dots will preen and primp over the vase and then these little fuckers will part like the Red Sea and, next thing you know, we'll all be singing carols together, exchanging stories, laughing by the fire.

And Dorothy Krause does open the gift, taking the box out of the royal gilded festive bag and placing it square on the countertop.

There it is now, the crystal vase, with roses etched on the side and, now for the kicker, the roses themselves, in the gift bag, waiting in the corner. Bright red roses for the glass rose vase. See. I thought it out.

The little brats are scurrying to get it all together, make it nice for Dotsy. Katy is cutting the flowers and arranging them in the vase, how nice, how pretty, just so.

"What a thoughtful gift. How gorgeous, these roses."

But somehow, even as they thank me they are shrinking back, pulling away from me, I am out of the circle. Something to be kept on the other side, something to be quarantined.

Maybe if I show the roses to the Lt. Colonel, maybe then there'll be the respect. These guys just don't know the pecking order, see? These guys just don't get it.

Reaching for the glass rose vase with new-cut scarlet roses, Shauna Boggs grabs it out of Katy's hands and holds it up from the kitchen, for the Lt. Colonel to see.

He's watching the game, third and goal in the fourth quarter, eyes glued to the screen, the announcer a delirium of hurried excitement. What's gonna happen? What's gonna happen? This could be the game . . . !

And from the other room, "Lt. Colonel? Lt. Colonel?! Look what I brought! Look at your present, for you and Dotsy!"

And the Lt. Colonel can hear noise and turn his head slightly, but that's all he can do, third and goal, fourth quarter, past the two-minute warning.

And Brad, Katy, Lars, and Danek can stand there, but that's all they can do, watching Shauna Boggs, they-call-her-the-blob, holding up the wet glass vase, teetering, water dripping down the side, from the newly cut fresh red roses.

And you can't reach out in time, how could you, to grab the slippery vase from Shauna Blobs teetering in her cheap black parka. You can't grab it in time, from the clumsy meat hands on that sloping meat body and so, as you all watch, standing there like perplexed shepherds, the crystal vase with Christmas crimson roses slips out of her piggy hands and onto the floor in a thousand little pieces and glass shards and glass shards with roses and red petals and thorns and thorns with glass shards and water shards and a deadening silence.

In the background, Favre makes the catch and the announcer squeals in ecstasy and Lambeau Field explodes in a fever pitch of yellow and green. But the Lt. Colonel is left out in the cold, sitting abandoned in the living room, a solitary figure, staring into the kitchen at the three-hundred-pound girl in a parka, a shuddering girl, suspended in glass shards and thorns and beaten-up roses.

FOUR

A mackerel sky in tendrils over the lake, the lake frozen over in white, tucked in from the lighthouses heralding Lake Michigan. Muskegon Lake ice fishing. Perch. Walleye. Northern pike. The best of the first and last ice pan-fish. Detective Samuel Barnett leaving early morning, 4 AM for blasted sakes, tiptoeing out, trying not to wake his wife breathing deep snug under the quilt.

Out on the lake, in his makeshift tin-pan shack with heater. A hole in the ice and nothing doing, sat freezing his ass off on the bench, nothing but this Old Style to keep him warm. Goddammit, he shoulda brought two sausage sandwiches, not just one. The wife had offered two, just in case, honey. But no, no, being a stupid little boy kid husband, not wanting to be that known, that predictable, he'd refused. Trying to play the man. And now starving, starving between these flimsy walls of aluminum grating, no more sausage sandwiches and not even noon, hell with it. What a dumb fuck. He might as well relent. The wife was right. Two sausage sandwiches, not just one.

Over the milk pebble sheet, a charcoal-black figure, a lone wanderer over the splat clear rink, coming closer, closer, closer, a gnat, then a cockroach, then a monkey, then a man. Now, a uniformed man outside the shack. A knock on the *rin-tin-tin* aluminum.

"Detective?!"

A sigh, what now. Can't I just have one day? Is that asking too much?

"Detective Barnett? You in there?"

Of course I'm in here, dumb-ass, where else would I be?

"Uh. Yeah."

"Can I come in?"

"Might as well."

A scutter and a clang off the *ting-ting* grating, careful of your feet, that ice is no joke. Breath now in vapor gusts, in-out in-out, vapor gasps made of words, out of breath, gushing.

"Detective, there's someone down at the station. Wants to talk to you."

"Well, it's Saturday—"

"I know. I know. That's what I said, sir. I sure did. But they wouldn't have it. Said it had to be you they talked to, wouldn't leave even."

"Well, what the hell?"

"You got that right, sir."

Air in puffs, made of ice.

"That sandwich place open?"

Heading back over Shoreline in the Ford Crown Vic, limited slip rear differential and boy do you need it. Even a barely there wisp cloud day like this the ground goes ice snow sludge slop pebbles ice again. You just never know what's down deep underneath.

The station empty, dark in mint-gray chrome, one fluorescent spotlight over the far chrome desk in green-gilled yellow. Sitting there, facing away, a fat-shirt with a bald head, one hair over the bald circle forehead wrong ways. His parka, forest green, draped over his lap. Nervous.

"Hi there."

"Hello. Hello, Officer."

"Nice day."

"Yes. Yes it is. Very nice day. No snow yet."

"Yup. That blizzard's coming in though, ought to be here tonight." Detective cozy-talk.

"Oh?"

"Yeah. They said three feet in Milwaukee, so . . . "

Better just sit down. Sit down, act casual, pretend to look through paperwork. Official.

"Detective. I have something to report."

Keep your eyes on the desk, act unmoved, calm. Professional.

"Some information."

"M-hm. M-hm. Go ahead."

"Well, it's just, uh. I saw that film. That one in town. On the girl. You know, the students did that film. And, um. I just thought, maybe . . . well, maybe there was something you should know."

Oh my Lord. Is this it? Is this the guy? Holy shit. Where's my gun?

"Oh, okay. Well, shoot."

Get out the pen and paper. Don't let him see. Keep him calm. Maybe it is him. A confession! Oh, fuck, where is my goddamn gun?

"Did I get your name? Sorry, I just, you know, I was ice fishing. Trying to catch some perch, bring home to the wife. And I, uh, guess I'm, well . . . still out there on the ice. Shame on me. What was, what was your name again?"

"Eric. Eric Walter. Um. I live down on Cheney. Down by the diner, off of Route 31."

"Oh, okay. CJ's, right. Is that a good diner? I drive by there all the time, always wanted to stop."

"Yeah, it's good. Real good. They got, uh, pierogis. Real good pierogis. The owner's wife's Russian, so . . . "

"Oh, that sounds good. My wife made some pierogis a couple months back."

Motioning to the rookie cop. Stay where you are. Stay put. Act casual. Don't leave. Don't make a fuss.

"It's just that. That girl. The Krause girl?"

"M-hm?"

"Well . . . I met her."

"M-hm."

Stay where you are, act normal. Nothing special.

"I met her a few days before she disappeared . . . before, you know . . . "

"M-hm."

"And I woulda come in. Woulda said something but . . . I tell you what, I was so damned scared somehow it'd get turned around and . . . all of a sudden I'd be the one, I'd be like a suspect . . . so . . . I just. You know, I just stayed put."

"Mm."

The green-muck light overhead. Rookie cop on the seat behind, metal seat, trying not to listen, trying to stay still.

"And well, I'm just. Well, I'm ashamed of myself. That I didn't come forward. Ashamed that. Maybe I coulda helped."

"M-hm."

"That poor girl. And her family and all. Seem like real nice people."

The buzz of the light overhead.

"And how did you come to meet her exactly?"

Careful now. Don't seem too interested. Don't scare him off.

"Well, it was. I mean, it was . . . it was late. It was a Friday night, late, and I was coming home from work. I got a store, up on Main. Walter's Tackle and Bait. That's my store. Maybe you been there?"

"I have been there! Sure have. Come to think of it, I think I got some hooks there last month. I always lose my hooks, you know. Every season the wife puts 'em away. Trying to keep things neat, I guess. And then I just lose them. Gotta buy 'em all over again. Wait a minute—are you in cahoots with my wife?"

A sly smile from rookie cop, from behind. A little laugh. Keep things light. Keep things easy here. Reel him in. Don't let him get away. Reel him in like that perch you missed out on.

"Oh, no sir. We run an honest business. Might not run too long though, with that Walmart and all . . . "

"Oh, I know. It's a shame, isn't it? Just a damn shame . . . So, it was late, you said?"

"Yeah, it was late, down on Route 31, down by Dreamers. And I was coming home, I see this girl and, I mean, it is cold outside, must be ten below. And, this girl is in nothing but a denim skirt and a pullover, walking down the road, stumbling even."

"M-hm. Down by Dreamers?"

"Yup. Well, I was worried about her, worried she'd freeze, out there like that. So, I gave her a ride."

"Uh-huh. Was she hitchhiking?"

"No. No, sir. She, she was just, well. She was drunk. I mean, she was a little girl, real petite and . . . I mean it was like . . . she didn't know where she was practically. Like it was all a joke or something."

"M-hm."

"And so, I mean, I couldn't even get out of her, you know, who she was, where she was going, her address. Nothing. And she just kept laughing. Real weird. Like laughing, cackling almost. And then crying. The next second. Just, back and forth. Just . . . crazy."

"Huh."

"I mean I couldn't tell if it was like . . . she was crazy or, you know, crazy drunk. But, I mean, she passed out. She just blacked out right there in the car."

"M-hm."

"And, I mean, I couldn't just leave her in the car, 'cause, well . . . I mean, she woulda froze."

"Uh-huh."

"So . . . I took her inside, took her home, put a blanket over her and just thought, you know, when she wakes up, when she sobers up, I'll just find out where she lives and take her home."

"You took her to your house?"

"Yessir. I did. I didn't know what else to do."

"Okay, and then . . . "

"Well, I woke up, real early, you know, to check up on her. And she was gone."

"Gone?"

"Yessir. She was just . . . gone."

"You mean like—"

"—Like she wasn't there. Like she split. And that woulda been, let's see, Saturday morning. Around six o'clock. Six AM."

"Six AM. Saturday."

"And then, a few days later, there I am watching the evening news. And there she is. Disappeared. Dead. And, well, I just . . . I mean, I just went white. I just, I just couldn't believe it."

"M-hm. I see. Well, we're gonna need a written statement. We can, uh, go through it with you, of course. If you don't mind. Just a formality, really."

"I understand. I understand, Officer."

"One more thing. Can you remember anything else? Anything else that might just stand out?"

"Well, yeah. There was one thing. She kept . . . she kept going on and on about this locket. Like she has this locket and she kept taking it out and crying even. I mean, and even when she went to sleep, she had it in her hands, like grasping it."

"Huh. Can you describe it, do you remember?"

"Yeah, it was a blue-and-white locket with a lady's face. Like a silhouette. Um . . . what is it called . . . a cameo?"

Outside the blizzard night air goes *whoosh whoosh whoosh*, sweeping past the windows, *swoop swoop swoop*. The windows tight but still knocking up against the frames. The blue wood bedroom at the top of the stairs, wife asleep beside Detective Samuel Barnett, arm tucked in around his waist. Conked out. How could she sleep through the *click clatter click* of the windowpanes, the *whoosh whoosh whoosh* of the wind? A champion sleeper, his wife. He envied her.

What soft, padded dreams lay out before her? What easy fluff clouds carried her away each night on a sea of calm, placid waves. A simple wife. Solid. Trying recipes, reading under the warm glow from the bedside lamp, always a blanket at her feet, to her waist. Packing up sandwiches, trying a new dessert off *Redbook*, sending their two daughters articles over the internet. Oh, how she loved the Internet. Always a new story, a new wonder, a new curiosity over the Internet. Always a new favorite thing, a new interest. Genuinely curious, his wife.

Nancy.

Genuinely, actively, happily digging up facts, cures, ideas, exclaiming upon a new discovery, exhilarated by a new find, a new study, a new invention. A lover of innovation. A lover of the future. A true optimist. How lucky he'd been to find her. How drizzly and lonely his life without her. Without her exclamations over a rump roast, her fake gasp over a vulgarity, her excitement over the latest Harry Potter book. "You know that J.K. Rowling, she was on welfare, you know."

Almost silly, in a way, his wife. But always knowing she was being silly. Always knowing she was being silly and being silly anyway. A choice not to be morose. A choice not to be self-serious.

People just liked her.

Nancy. The kind of wife who got on with anyone from rookie cop to the professors down at Hope. Always something funny to say, always some common ground to say it. Never judgmental. Never rude. An easygoing kind of wife. Easily judged as simple but not simple. As time goes by, complicated even.

Every once in a while, a strange sort of surprise thing coming out of her mouth. An off thing. A sharp and macabre kind of thing you'd never expect. No, there was wit and acumen underneath that brisket-baking exterior. She chose to be happy. That was the thing with her. She knew it was easy to fall apart, how easy it could be. But, simple, silly and strong. His wife. A goofy rock. A why-not foundation.

Rolling over in the *clack-clack* storm, her arm burrowing itself under the pillow.

"Honey, what? Why are you up? It's late."

"Thinking about this case. This guy came in today. Said he met her."

"Hm."

"Said she was drunk. The Friday before. Said she was laughing and crying, crazy."

"Hm. Sounds like love. You should ask her friend."

"Huh?"

"Her friend. That Boggs girl. Bet she'd know."

SIX

Coming off the shift at Smart-tek, an eight-hour day, starting at dawn, Shauna in a brick wool sweater and jeans, galoshes, heading out through the bite-your-face wind to her champagne-color Nissan, Detective Barnett trying to fake a casual encounter, a surprise even in the cement lot shared with RadioShack, Payless, Applebee's.

Over the wind, or into the wind, "Shauna? Shauna Boggs?"

And yes, that's her, Shauna Boggs in the giant cherry pullover, lumbering Shauna Boggs making her way over the slush slush snow lot to her champagne sleigh, a sad-sack Santa, in fire-engine red.

"Shauna. How funny! I was just thinking about you!"

A stop in the snow, not a turn. Let me go. Leave me alone.

"It's me. Detective Barnett. Remember? We met . . . way back, oh when was it . . . ?"

And turning now, a face to greet, a flush-face force-smile for the nice officer. A cheery run-in. Oh, yes, what a coincidence! How long do I have to feign interest? Is this enough? Please make this enough.

"Oh. Hi. Didn't see you there."

"I'm sorry. Jeez. Hope I didn't scare you. Hey, you know, I had a few things I wanted to ask you. Just a few quick questions. If you don't mind."

"What? Here?"

Looking around the North Pole sheet, the gale of wind sweeping through the parking lot, a concrete canal, a wind tunnel of commerce.

"No, no. How stupid. How 'bout . . . what about over here . . . I'll buy you a drink. Some coffee maybe?"

Pointing out the Applebee's. This very special, unlike any other Applebee's on earth. Inside, a family crowd, a high-chair crowd, a night out with the folks.

And Shauna, nodding glib, "Sure. Sure thing."

Ass-aching from these hours and hours, at Smart-tek, ear glued to the phone. Dawn 'til dusk, nighttime now, skip daylight. Smart-tek for a smart future! What a bowl of shit.

The menu at Applebee's, a pornography of food. A baked potato vagina in close-up, oozing sour cream. A roast beef sandwich spread wide open, red dripping juice. Eat me fuck me eat me. A Polish sausage bursting between two heaving buns, lick me suck me lick me. An x-rated cornucopia of burgers, buns, poppers, wings, tanglers, riblets, sliders. And suddenly, Shauna famished.

"Order whatever you want, I'm hungry, too, actually."

And Shauna would, and Shauna did.

"I'll have a double cheeseburger, mushroom-styled, with fried onions, onion rings instead of fries, and an Oreo cookie shake. Oh, and also the southwestern chili to start."

The crying of babies seemingly from every corner, bouncing

off the Kelly-green and burgundy booths, walls, molding. Molding at the Applebee's. Nothing but the best.

Balloons, stripes, high-chairs, baby wailing, Mom cooing, Dad checking out the game. A big game tonight, Vikings versus the Bears. All husband eyes on the screen. All wife eyes on baby and toddler but not on kid. Poor kid, no eyes on you anymore. You grew up. Eat your vegetables.

"Oh, and an Applebeetini, please."

"Sure thing, ma'am."

Ma'am! How she hated to be a ma'am. How she missed being a young lady, a miss. Miss? You left your umbrella. Miss? You dropped your keys. How she missed those lusty, devouring eyes. People used to pay to fuck me, you know! But now, the dull and terminal ma'am, grunted out with a resounding thud. Ma'am. It's over. Ma'am, you don't exist.

Can't eat enough to get through this so-called chance encounter, can't put this, those, that in my mouth fast enough. More, more, more! I'll have dessert. That Peanut Buster Parfait Banana Boat inspired by Dairy Queen. Maybe that. What about you? How 'bout the key lime pie? Oh, I'll try that. If you get it, I mean. I'll have a bite.

"Shauna, do you remember anything unusual about the week before the incident . . . the weekend before?"

"Mm. Hmm? Let me think . . . "

Peanut Butter Parfait over a fudge-filled chocolate brownie. Mile-High Ice Cream Pie! Triple Chocolate Meltdown! Sinful. Chocolate always sinful. Chocolate always out of reach, a temptation. Cheat! Cheat with me, with chocolate. Decadent, oozing chocolate. Gobble me up, satisfy your darkest urges, your deep dark chocolate cravings, come to me, an ecstasy in chocolate.

"Not really, Detective. It was so long ago . . . "

People are beginning to stare. Even here. Even during the third quarter of the Bears against the Vikes, staring at the three-hundred-pound girl wolfing down fudge. The nice charcoal detective, concerned, dignified. Here he is with an Old Style and, I swear, that's her fourth Applebeetini. Swear to God. Yes, four.

"Anything about that Friday night before?"

"Um. Let me see . . . "

Applebeetinis can go swirl in your head. Oh, the game's on. Go, Bears! I hate those fucking Vikes. Everyone knows the Lions suck anyway, gotta root for someone.

"No, I just . . . I really can't re-mehm-ber."

"No problem. I understand. I know it was a long time ago. Gosh, you know, feels like yesterday sometimes."

"Yeah. Kinda does."

The words coming out strange, not coming out on the consonants. Put the words on the consonants, Shauna. Put 'em back.

"Yes. I mean. It. Kind. Of. Does. Feel that way."

Jesus, get a hold of yourself. People are staring, whispering, not the babies, not the toddlers. The wives. The kids. The kids have nothing to do but that Fun-4-Kids placemat. A search-a-word, a treasure map, a word scramble. Too easy. They must make these things for slow kids. Crayons make it come to life. Crayons make your kids shut the fuck up.

"Do you remember . . . that place called Dreamers? That bar? Do you remember Beth saying something about going there?"

Fuck, man, what's wrong with my mouth? It's not that hard to say it. Dreamers. Dream-ers. There, I said it. Jesus.

"Do you remember anything about a locket? A locket she had?"

"You know, Officer. Detective . . . Barnett. Beth was a real sweet girl . . . real kind, you know. She . . . "

A wash of DeKuyper Luscious Red Apple emotion, an Applebeetini lament, spilling over now, a green apple tsunami. A pucker gone sour.

"She just didn't deserve that. Any of it. She was really . . . sweet, you know."

And tears now, coming down that pink pudge face, those swine-slit eyes. Applebeetini tears down into the green apple sob, slobbering, shoulders shaking. Misery at the Applebee's! A spectacle over blooming onions.

And the wives tell their kids not to stare, and the babies coo and the toddlers goo and the husbands watch the game and never care.

SEVEN

Dreamers, during the day more of a nightmare. Coming in from the bright light glare off the snow and the sky, and into Dreamers, a cave with a black-and-white check floor. Plum walls, red walls, walls covered in beer signs, Polaroids, bottles over mirrored glass, gleaming from behind the bar like gems. Bottle diamonds. Kill-you jewels.

At the end of the bar, two old swill-faces, one in a ski vest, one in a flannel. Scotch and soda for each. Shaky age-spot hands reach for the scotch glass, bring it up, bring it up shaking, barely, to the grand release from memory, snuggling up to oblivion. A forget-me sip. A forget-me life. I am done here.

How many stories, Detective Barnett wondered, end up here, end up told here. Stories about the one that got away, stories about the chances, missed opportunities, could-have-beens? How many dreams died down here at Dreamers? Where the elixir embrace replaces the arms, hands, lips, of Jenny from back home, Julie from high school, all the things I did to fuck it up with Jean.

A woman barfly, a rarer species. Seldom seen. Where were they? At home, drinking alone, watching TV, sneaking bottles?

But surely there were as many male ones as well, doing the same? Was it dead even? Or were there simply more of the lost male flies on bar stools? This losing species? This non-function, never to replace itself, never to replicate? Dying out, this breed, maybe. Single, splat-faced, alone, listening to talk radio, complaining about the media, the government, the way this country's headed, you ought to be scared. Why not more lady barflies? Was there something in a woman, some survival mechanism, latched on to production, reproduction, replication, what is solid, what is here, what is before them? A house? A child? A man? A place to live? Food to eat? Bread on the table? Like Nancy. His wife. Pragmatic. Choosing to be happy. Choosing not to dwell.

This place was full of dwellers. They should change the name to Dwellers.

Dreamers!

Ha.

Now that is a good one.

Behind the bar, a mid-twenties belly-scratch in black scruffy hair and stubble. A bear of a kid but you could see how he'd pull.

"Anything I can do for you, Officer?"

"Detective. Detective Barnett. I'll have a coffee, if you got it."

"Sure thing."

The blotch-faces at the end of the bar turning, slight, away, from the cop. Don't look at me. Don't look at me, I am not here. I don't exist. Don't make me.

Behind the bar, a smattering of pictures, from floor to ceiling, Polaroids, digital pics printed out thin, hundreds, maybe thousands of let-your-hair-down nights, wild girl times, guys in packs, girls red-faced, even lifting up their shirts. Look at me. Look how crazy. Look what I'll do! Love me.

Could be '70s, '80s, '90s, now, an eternity of waste-face nights, passed out next to the toilet, dancing on the bar, Super Bowl Sunday, Red Wings tailgate, Oktoberfest, St. Patrick's Day everybody in green hats, green beer, Kiss Me I'm Irish pins and T-shirts.

And then, this one.

"Can I see that?"

"Which one, over here?"

"Yeah, no, that one. That one there."

Belly bartender reaches back. "This one?"

"Yeah, that's it. Can I see that?"

"Fine with me. Kinda old anyways."

Shrugging, he hands it over. Might as well keep it.

An almost black Polaroid in the bathroom. A schoolgirl smile, we're doing something bad. We're doing something bad, aren't we? A brown-haired, dough-skinned girl in red halter, sitting on the sink, leaning forward, looking into the camera. At the man behind the camera. I know you want to fuck me. I know you do. Maybe I'll let you. Maybe.

Shauna Boggs.

Twenty-one. Maybe twenty-two.

And, around her neck, a blue-and-white Wedgwood locket.

A cameo.

EIGHT

They'll never find who dropped it off. They'll never find who left it.

In fact, the box, the little beige or gray or white dingy box sitting there, first at the back of the station, then under a desk, and finally on top of a desk, behind the DETECTIVE BARNETT placard, would take two weeks to make that journey.

Two weeks in which something had happened to the respected, well-liked, assuring yet still irreverent detective, who couldn't stop sitting at his desk, staring at pictures.

Here's his favorite picture to watch. A photograph of the front office of the Green Mill Inn. The chintzy little safe, a safe for a child, really, is pried open . . . its contents on the floor. A few coins, papers, the rest gone. The paperwork, bills, documents, and a muscle-car calendar are all flayed out on the ground, spread. The chair, knocked over. The clock, broken, froze at 8:45. The phone, a green dial phone, off the hook. Of course.

What Detective Barnett watched in this picture, what drew his eye, what he stared at waiting to coagulate behind his ears, was this:

It was too perfect.

That is . . . too deliberate. It looked, if you looked closely, like a crime scene you'd see on a TV movie of the week. Straight out of production. The phone, the papers strewn, the chair, the safe . . . all just so. A child's rendering of a break-in.

But why would there be so much astray when the object was simply the safe? Wouldn't you, if you were breaking into some shit-ass motel in the freezing cold of March, just go straight for the safe and be done with it? Why mess around with the chair, the papers, the clock, the phone . . . ?

Signs of a struggle.

Yes, there had to be signs of a struggle.

But why?

The girl, Beth Krause, was no more than five-foot-three, maybe a hundred pounds, soaking wet in a snowsuit. She was slight. A butterfly.

With her, there would be no struggle. You would just fling her aside and that would be that. Christ, you could hold her off with one arm if you wanted.

So, why the Herculean, all-too-purposeful attempt to create, to display, a "sign of the struggle"?

It came between picking up his mug and pouring in his coffee, as these things always do, a stabbing thought. In its wake, a shirtsleeve full of coffee and a reaching for a pen. Never mind the coffee, who gives a shit about the coffee now. Now it's just this!

The safe was not the object of the crime, nor the money from the safe.

The girl was the object of the crime.
The girl was not the afterthought.
The girl was the thought.
They knew her.

NINE

They'll never find who dropped it off. They'll never find who left it.

That grubby little box. A shoe box, blank. All alone, poor box, in that rackety rickety station house. A study in green and gray. Metal everything, desks, trash cans . . . bars. Metal even in the windows. Tile floors, green and gunmetal gray. And then, in the midst with papers and walking and mumbled words at the end of a long day . . . still that box, all by its lonesome. Sitting there. Dynamite.

"Uh, boss, I think you might want to take a look at this."

He's a young cop. Neophyte. Rooky. Sweet kid. Barnett wondered if he'd make it, all heart like that.

It would be this moment, opening that once pristine, now muddled box, that Detective Barnett would go to his grave thinking of. How had it come to pass? Who had left it? And why? And, let's face it, how goddamned lucky it had been.

There she was.

A Polaroid story.

That beautiful, innocent, choir-singing girl, Beth Krause . . . not so innocent now, is she?

Both she and, in this one, another girl. Parts of girls. Girl parts. Girl parts not supposed to be in pictures. Splices of meat. Slabs. Polaroid pieces, bites out of girls.

Who is this other Beth Krause?

Look at her!

And then, in this set of photographs, it's a party. A different party, a different night, a different outfit, a different season, a different man.

And there is Beth Krause in this one, a white tank top and denim skirt. It's a bar, there she is, sitting on his lap, and then his lap . . . arms around his neck and then his and then his. Smiling. Sly. Sexy. Slurred.

I have all of you in the palm of my hand.

And I know it.

The background in these next ones, a room, a familiar room. Rooms. All the same. Slightly different rooms of the hotel, same bedspreads, same carpet, same windows, different sofa, different art.

Same low ceilings. Same crappy over-lit, green-gilled lighting.

Same bathroom. White gilly-white. A light-box square.

And here . . . in this one, what's her name, that girl . . . Troy's kid. Shauna. Shauna Boggs.

(Before she gained weight . . . before they started calling her around town, he knew, Shauna Blobs. And then, years later, Shauna Blob. And now, finally, simply, definitively, the Blob. What was she now, three hundred pounds . . . Christ, he couldn't imagine it. Poor girl.)

And there the younger, thinner Shauna Boggs smiles. In this

one, hair down. In this one, hair in a bun. This one, hot, sweaty, a macramé sundress. Summer.

In this one, boots, plaid skirt, a blazer. Fall.

In this one, red and green tinsel in the background. Someone's holding the mistletoe. Will she give him a kiss? Please? Pretty please? Christmas. Shauna's mouth is open, laughing rough.

And on and on, past the bright shiny hats and streamers. FIVE . . . FOUR . . . THREE . . . TWO . . . ONE! HAPPY NEW YEAR!!

1978.

Strung up in gold purple red across the door.

Past Valentine's Day . . . hearts. Shauna Boggs is wearing a red sweater. She has lots of valentines. In this picture . . . five. Five men surround her, their eyes greedy. That hot pink skirt of hers. Eat her up! Oh, please, will you please be my valentine. Gobble me up.

The men, older. Late twenties. Maybe thirty. This one in the background could be forty. Gray around the temples. But this one, with the deep-set eyes . . . twenty-eight, maybe twenty-nine . . . in almost all the pictures.

Either near Shauna Boggs and looking confident, boastful, vulgar, or far . . . looking away. Looking for what exactly?

In this one, there she is on the lap of a dirt-haired man in a Jethro Tull T-shirt. And over here, the deep-set man . . . look at his hands clasped tight, knuckles white. He stares frozen at the door, who is he expecting?

But here, even more unfathomable, a happy Shauna Boggs, all those years ago. Swaying at the bar. Maybe Dreamers. Next to her friend. Beth. There's a pool table and blossom-faces all around. The center of all the fuss. Miss Beth. Everybody's sweetheart. Little miss perfect. She is clasping her hands over a Wedgwood locket, a white cameo face over blue.

They knew her.

TEN

A wet, overcast noon in the comedown days of January. Above in the milk-gray muddle of clouds, a wash of clouds, an unblinking sun, stares down through a blown-out yellow glaze, through the opaque screen.

Below this sullen canopy, a lone figure in a dark gray uniform stares, hesitant, at the edge of the sidewalk, newly shoveled. The snow in piles off the sidewalk, little crest of dirt ridges near the tops, a buildup of snow since November, pebbles in the snow, snow-flecked pebbles, snow dirt, dirt in snow, old snow slush, snow turned into ice and then back again.

Detective Samuel Barnett did not want to make this visit. Earlier this morning, in bed there next to his wife, she'd dragged her fingers through his hair, reassuring.

"It'll be fine. They'll understand."

Not wanting to leave, wanting to stay there next to his warm-skinned, quilt-wrapped wife, home, tucked in safe.

"They know you, Samuel. They'll understand."

And now, standing here at the end of this walkway, wanting nothing more than to get back in his black-and-white, made-in-America Crown Vic, drive home, climb up the stairs and back under the covers. She'll be there reading, now, probably, bundled up under the covers.

Step by step down the walkway. It's not too late to go back. You could just go back now, they'd never know you were here. Quick. Hurry. Go back. Now's the time. Just forget it.

Knocking on the door, he had the sensation of somebody else knocking. That must be somebody else's wrist, somebody else's hand, knuckles, making those sounds. *Tap tap tap.*

What if he left now? He could still get away. Maybe they wouldn't even hear it. He didn't knock that loud. He could just go. Go. And it'd be done. That's that. Just drop the whole thing.

There's a press on the door, from the other side, a moment, and then, presto, door open. Door is now open and, on the other side, in an apron with an apple on the front, apples on the side, up to the bow, Dorothy Krause.

"Oh. Hello. Detective."

A moment of too many words to say. How to say it? What does it mean that you're here? Can't be good. Can't be good that you're here, Detective, right? We both know it. Too old to hide it, too. Too old for cover-ups.

"Mrs. Krause. I'm sorry to bother you. Um. I hope I didn't come at a bad time."

Cop speak. Yes, it's cop speak, but what else is there? He can't just blurt it out.

Dotsy, standing there, wiping the flour off her hands with a dish towel.

"No, no. That's fine. Come in, you must be freezing."

Trying to make it nice.

"Maybe you can try my new recipe. Blueberry crumble muffins. It's new. I just don't know if I got it right. This old oven."

Walking though the frost-blue house, no more Christmas decorations, just taken down.

"We should probably replace it but, you know, such a hassle."

At the table sits the Lt. Colonel, reading the newspaper, in front of him a cup of coffee, toast, and a slice of braunschweiger.

"Lt. Colonel. Hello there. Sorry to bother you."

And the Lt. Colonel, military haircut, stands and says nothing. The detective here, no, no that can't be good. Something soon to upset. Something soon to rattle. Brace yourself.

"Please, let's . . . Do you mind if we sit?"

Detective Samuel Barnett trying to find the words. Oh God. Why can't I be home under the quilt? Why do I have to do this today? And what if I'm wrong. Jesus. What then?

"Detective, how about some coffee? I bet you could use some coffee and maybe a muffin? Sit down, take off your coat. Honey, more coffee?"

The Lt. Colonel shakes his head no and now they are sitting there at the dining room table. Next to the dining table, a picture window and, outside, a scene fit for a still life. The black tree branches, snow-covered, the snow-covered yard, the bird feeder dressed in snow, a sliver oval of ice float water and next to it, now, a robin.

"American robin. Fairly common."

The Lt. Colonel assures the detective.

"Yesterday we had a cardinal. Beautiful thing."

"That's right, next to the snow, bright red, I tried to get my camera but . . . "

Now Dotsy coming in, a plate of muffins, oatmeal cookies, and shortbread, a doily on the plate. Everything just right. Everything just so. Done the old way. From the old time. "All homemade. Except the shortbread. The shortbread is just that same Walkers."

Now the three of them are seated at the dining table, the tablecloth pale blue and cream. A casual everyday tablecloth, across it an ivory lace runner. In the middle a bowl of fruit, a Willow Ware bowl with apricots and apples.

The robin outside drinks and looks around, drinks and looks around, then a little hop, then a drink, hop hop hop.

"Delicious. Delicious muffins. What did you say they were?"

"Blueberry crumble. It's a new recipe. From *Redbook*."

"Well, I'll have to get it, for my wife. She'd like that."

"Oh, that's easy. I'll just jot it down. The secret is blueberries. You can get 'em at the farmers market, fresh."

The robin looks around, hop hop, drinks under the wan washed sky.

"Well, as you might have guessed, well . . . there's been some renewed interest in the case. Your daughter's case. Since the documentary."

Not wanting to speak. Not wanting to say it. Maybe he could just say forget it and still get away, a fluke of a visit, no big deal. It wasn't too late. Last chance. Just drop it.

"And, um, well, there have been some new developments. In the case."

The Lt. Colonel reaches his hand over, past the coffee, past the paper, past the muffins, and puts his hand on Dotsy's wrist, now trembling.

Dotsy's lips are pressed together, her eyes staring down at the table.

"And, well, this, this isn't easy. Well, Lt. Colonel, Dorothy . . . we have reason to believe we may actually be able to solve this case. Now. With the kind of technology available today. Um. DNA testing. In particular. We think, maybe, given the right amount of information, the right tests, we might be able to get the matter resolved, finally."

They are waiting. They are suspended. There is a question coming here.

"And, in this case, that would mean to get the right information . . . we would have to . . . um . . . get permission from the two of you to . . . well . . . exhume the body."

Dotsy's eyes close. Keep them closed.

Outside the picture window the orange-chested robin goes hop hop hop, takes a drink, and then hop, gone away for good. And now the birdbath and the white blanket lawn and the black scraggle trees bury their heads in sorrow, suddenly alone, abandoned, and the desolate postcard wants no more to be looked at.

ELEVEN

The white laid out over the sloping hill, the sun just above the horizon in a yellow glow glare. Never gold, on a freeze black-tree silent morning like this. Fifteen below windchill and the tombstones sticking out of the milk-sprawl ground, sporadic. No grid here. As random the plots as the snow around them. Some trodden. Lots of visitors. Some bare as an ice rink. No visitors. Long dead. What did you make of it? Does it matter now? What did you collect? Anything good? Is it with you now?

Some buried in great grand family orchestrations, with giant granite obelisks. Fischer. Macon. Collins. We were in it together. We were a family. We meant something. Once. Some, just the two of them, husband and wife. We stayed true. We fall and rise as one.

Then, also, the lone gravestones with nothing around, no prints, nothing but the scrape-black trees and the shadows drawing long in rectangles for companionship. What did it mean, any of it? What did I do wrong, to end up alone and snow-print-less here? Or do we all end up alone, really?

Then, the angel field near the gates, reserved for toddlers, infants, and children. The ground crying, too. Don't fill me. Don't fill me with that.

And all beneath the pale, oatmeal sky with streaks of silver, streams of yellow-white strands masking sunrise. Wake up!

But no one will wake up here. A stubborn lot. The granite making stretch square shadows down the snow field. Limitless silence. A thousand questions to each stone square. No answer.

The hill slopes up from the west to the east and there, near the top, a flurry of activity around a giant orange monster, a metal dinosaur up early, grazing the grounds. A winter morning peace-killing involving five men, three squad cars, a Caterpillar, and a beige morgue van crowded around, buzzing, digging, pausing in front of, behind.

Elizabeth Lynn Krause

June 21, 1956 - March 13, 1978

Detective Samuel Barnett had made a visit to this cemetery, Mayview, on his fortieth birthday with his wife rolling her eyes throughout the ordeal. It was a lark, really, they'd been driving through the outskirts of town, deciding between restaurants for the evening. She'd wanted French. Mes Amis on Main. He'd wanted steak. Carter's off Fairfield. Somehow, the green grass of Mayview had summoned him through the wrought-iron gates that lazy afternoon in June.

No sooner had they turned in over the gravel dirt road carving its way through the headstones than the conversation switched suddenly from mussels to burial plots. Nancy had thought the whole thing was foolish. A macabre excursion on your birthday! But the detective had persevered, walking the grounds, finding a nice area near the east side of the slope, the top of the hill, underneath an enormous elm. A tree trunk the size of a bathtub, spread out over the grassy slope, protective.

He'd mapped the plots, marched down to the office and bought them both on a whim. One for him, one for Nancy. You can never be too sure.

The woman on duty, a milquetoast of seventy in a gold-button navy-blue blazer, had thought it odd, too. What did it mean? These two buying plots on his fortieth birthday? Was this some sort of cry for help? A murder–suicide? What to make of it? But there was nothing to make of it, sure. The wife seemed cheerful, chiding her husband, calling him morbid. Chipper in her reprimands. No, no, it was fine. Just a husband being absurd. Trying to get a rise out of his wife. He loved her, you could tell.

It was strange, though, how he'd insisted on the Super-Deluxe Peaceful for Eternity package, treatment, tombstones, service and weekly-flower-arrangement option. It ain't cheap. Rich people had scoffed at the price, even. And for a cop . . . it did seem extravagant.

Even his wife thought it extensive.

"What does it matter, honey. We certainly won't notice."

But, in this as in all things, he'd dug his heels in. No explanation. The Super-Deluxe it was. And would always be, for eternity.

That plot, those two plots, for future, for he and Nancy were not far, only thirty feet about, from this plot, this past plot, marked Elizabeth Lynn Krause, rest in peace.

And peace, well. Not here with the dig-dig Caterpillar, bright orange against the white sheet grade. On the side CATERPILLAR in big black capitals, the only black other than the leafless trees, all watching. What's this? What's all this, this morning?

"Well, boss, there they are."

And, turning to look, there they were, indeed. Outside the redbrick awning and wrought Mayview gates, lined up on Mayview Drive, the inevitable, complacent, stodgy pale vans with UFO antennas on top, circling around for a signal.

"Goddamn news. Buncha vultures."

Detective Barnett had thought this pre-morning, just-dawn excursion might throw them off, but even as he turned, there they were, scurrying toward him through the snow. One in an emerald suit dress and heels. Heels! In this snow. One in cargo pants holding the camera, clamoring over the gravestones toward him, barely audible, just within earshot and getting louder, inescapable.

"Detective! Detective!! What do you hope to find this morning? What do you hope to uncover? Have there been any new developments? Is it possible you missed something, Detective, back then, when you were a rookie?"

That last one an ice-pick stab through the eyes.

And behind him, the Caterpillar roaring, stop go stop go start dig, the giant orange claw eating into the snow, devouring the dirt.

Detective Barnett blindsided in the snowdrift. Oh Lord, please don't let me lose my job. Please let me be right. Please don't let me lose my job for this. And then: Well, if I do lose it, at least I got the Super-Deluxe Peace for Eternity package. Bought and paid for.

TWELVE

A midnight light of metal and blue, reflecting tables and cabinets, mirrored surfaces. A nighttime fun-house off limits to the public. A secret retreat from the crowds. The room made green from an overhead fluorescent light, industrial light, light to perform surgery. Death-surgery, after-surgery, death-light on a body decomposed.

You would have to cover your mouth and nose here. There was no way around it. No time to be brave. Cover up.

The coroner in lab coat and glasses, a diminutive, balding man who'd chosen a life of cutting open skin, cutting lines and looking in, a shut-in. A shut-in, excited now, having called the detective at a too-late time. An after-hours revelation, can't hold it in.

"Detective. Detective Barnett?"

Back at the house, the flannel sheets can't cover up the noise.

"Hold on. Hold up a second."

Tiptoeing out of bed, into the hallway. Don't wake the wife.

"Detective Barnett. I think you better come down here."

"You know what time it is?"

"I know. I know, but I just—I thought you'd want to see this."

Detective Barnett closing his eyes. Christ. This would be the last year. Maybe. Twelve after midnight and now you call.

The autopsy room housed in the basement. A floor of seafoam tiles, walls of ivory. Every table a silver slab, the light buzz a drone. Come in. Come in through the glass doors. Come in. Look here.

On the table, under the fish-gill light, a white sheet laid over, thank God. Cover your mouth, cover your nose, cover your eyes.

The bald head leading him to the microscopes. A presentation. Slides of glass with labels, DNA, hair, saliva, specimens, put them under the lens. Look. Look here.

"This, Detective, this is what I wanted you to see."

PART IV

ONE

Shauna didn't mind coming back to the Green Mill Inn, she'd gotten fired but who gives a fuck. Beth was here and that's all that mattered. She'd gotten her the job, why shouldn't she be here? Anyway the boss only came round on Fridays.

What did she care if little miss nitwit worked here now? She could just imagine her daydreaming her shift away. That was all Beth did . . . daydream. Wander around, lollygag by the railroad tracks. Dreaming. Singing. Doodling. Tethered ever so softly to this world, always seeming one heel here and one tiptoe into the next. Teetering soft between streetlights and thunderheads.

An apparition.

A lily-face.

A never-was-here-after-all.

She would do whatever Shauna wanted, whatever she asked. When they were together, Shauna had the power. Simply by degrees, by sheer fact, of being of this earth. Here. Feet firmly on the ground.

Where Beth could be found floating halfway to space . . . Shauna would reach up and grab her down. Come back. Come here. Let me teach you this earth language, these rules of engagement.

And you would think Beth would be grateful but she exhibited no signs of it. Anymore than an ant would be grateful not to be killed. No, she had no idea. Didn't care. Didn't seem interested, really.

The world outside her head, her eyes, was a mystery. A confusion. But nothing to be marveled at. Any more than you would marvel at a pit of mud. Yes . . . it held secrets . . . but no allure.

In this way, it was easy to hold down the fort in this brown wooden office for eight hours straight. Quite simply, she wasn't there.

Yes, the phone would ring but at that moment she'd be in Africa. She'd answer the phone but even that was a play of its own. Now the phone is in Dubai! Now I must answer before three rings, or the sultan will die!

Yes, a customer would come in, but at that moment, she'd be in Nepal. Of course she'd answer all the questions, give change for the soda machine, but really she was giving directions up the mountain, charge for the Sherpa, knowing full well they'd never make it down Everest.

In this way, all the world was at play for Beth Krause, revealing itself in shatter clouds and dialogue overheard—a face there, a name there—but never anything too detailed. Never anything bolted to the ground. She had always lived in the sky. And if she was inside, the sky was one wall away, just a ceiling—easily removed, a tin box around her—lift it up.

She never really saw Shauna, or her boss, or anyone.

She had a habit of giving everything away. It mystified her mother until she saw the good in it. It never ceased to amaze

Beth, the delight in someone's face over a knickknack, a throw-away, a trinket. None of these things meant anything to her but they meant so much to someone else, how could she not give them away?

Leaning in over the metal mint reception desk, Shauna took a conspiratorial tone.

"I got a secret."

"Here we go . . . " Beth breathing out.

"No, I do . . . I got a secret and you're gonna die."

Shauna had been saying something but what? It didn't matter. It was an endless series of dramas with her. A moment's theater. A fight. A rage. An indulgence. And then nothing. A constant scratch at the top of the coffin, buried deep underground. A hopeless, aimless desperation. A fury.

"Don't you want to know his name?"

"Whose name?"

"My guy."

"What guy?"

"My *boy*friend."

Shauna was wearing a purple top with orange, pink, blue, red stripes. No shoulders. A drawstring around the neck, keeping it up. Just. If she had a mother she would not be wearing that top.

Also, no bra. Just straight-down breasts, not too large but certainly not insignificant. Not enough to be without a bra. Beth wouldn't be caught dead with her breasts swooping around like that.

Provocative.

But wasn't that Shauna's defining characteristic? Hadn't she built her reputation, her following, her standout under that sheer unapologetic ability to push the buttons of anyone and everyone around her? I am here! I will not be ignored!

Beth's parents did not like Shauna Boggs. Although they were kind enough to hide it. Besides, she was someone to be looked after. A girl her age with no mother and a reprobate father. They couldn't exactly despise her. Certainly not more than she despised herself.

And the pushing.

"Okay, I'll give you one guess."

"Shauna, seriously?"

It was nearing the end of her shift and Beth was really just wishing she could get back to her crossword puzzle. She would finish it before she clocked out. She was like that. Everything in its place. The thing was nearly complete except the left top corner—she hadn't cracked it. 20 Down. Affliction. Six letters.

"Guess!"

"Um . . ."

Beth was wearing a light-blue Gunne Sax, one she had begged her mother, Dorothy, to buy for months. It was half the reason she got this job. She didn't want to have to beg like that ever again. Not for a Gunne Sax.

"Let's see. How about . . . Christopher?"

"Christopher?!"

"Christopher's a nice name. What's wrong with Christopher?"

"It's a twerp name. I'd never go out with a guy named Christopher, let alone call him my boyfriend."

"Okay, well, I give up."

Not exasperated, just bored. Beth wasn't in the mood for this anyway. Why did she even bother? Sometimes she wondered what the point was in having friends anyway. Six letters. Affliction. Third letter L.

"Jeff!"

"Mm."

"Jeff Cody."

"Mm-hm."

Beth tried to sound interested. Ancient dweller. Italy. Ends in N. Why was Shauna even talking now? Wasn't it obvious she didn't care? The whole thing stretched out before her like an endless white sheet. Nothing dulled the senses like the facts. Beth found herself looking for an excuse to get rid of Shauna and this mind-numbingly drab conversation. Get back to the corner. Six letters. 20 Down.

"Look. I kinda got to get started on these receipts."

"What receipts?"

"Oh, uh . . . they got me doing some bookkeeping so—"

"Bookkeeping? They never asked me to do any bookkeeping."

Always on defense.

Always on alert.

"Oh? Well, it's probably just they got sick of it . . . "

"Yeah, well, have at it. Besides. I have a date . . . with Jeff."

Squinting at the paper, tapping the pen, Beth didn't see him come in. But he saw her.

Standing there, beside Shauna, now beaming with pride, at over six feet, in black Judas Priest iron-on and oil-stained blue jeans . . . this must be Jeff.

Funny how she doesn't notice him. Still. Head in the desk.

Shauna can't stand it. She clears her throat. Look at me! Look at my man!

Beth looks up at the great Jeff with the dark brown hair and thick eyebrows and thinks, a fleeting thought, my poor best friend, this guy will break your heart into pieces.

hristmas 1976. Bicentennial Christmas.

Couldn't help but fall for the Christmas village, Christmas town set up down Main Street. The lights strung up over the snow-filled street, a Christmas tree at the end, little wooden stands set up like back home, back in Germany, *gluhwein*, glogg, mulled wine, spiced wine with brandy, cloves, orange peel, cinnamon, gulp it down and keep warm. Drink the *gluhwein*, walk around under the little sparkling lights, white, blue, red, green, twinkling magic lights at 4:30, just got dark and already night.

Beth Krause rushing out of the Macy's, the black suede that'll-be-the-day boots wrapped up, wrapped up in red for Shauna, her best friend, least she could do for Christmas. A big burgundy bow on the box, oh she couldn't wait to see.

But how could she not get them for Shauna, her best friend since grade school, after seeing her face light up at the boots, turn them over and fall blank, unanswered, at the price. Sure they were expensive, of course they were . . . but it was Christmas. Muskegon, Michigan, sparkling lights down Main Street and a Santa set up in Macy's. You couldn't help but get carried away.

She'd bought her mom a framed Maxfield Parrish print from

that antiques store down on Halpern. For Dad, it was harder, but she'd finally decided on an autographed framed Bart Starr black-and-white, she'd managed to get off one of her old classmates at Hope. She couldn't wait 'til he opened it. Maybe next year she'd find a way to finagle tickets to Lambeau. She knew it was hard, impossible almost but, you know, where there's a will, there's a way and it'd be worth it just to see his face. Oh my good Lord, he would flip! She made a note to try it, might have to start looking right away, come to think of it.

Making her way down Main Street, through the park and over to Shauna's. It was a long walk, sure, but it wasn't too cold yet and the snow hadn't started to come down. If she hurried, she could make it. Drop the present off and be home by six. Wasn't supposed to start coming down 'til seven, maybe eight.

Walking away, the Christmas village behind, she had a feeling of falling off somehow, coming off the roller coaster ride, retreating. The Christmas carols and the *ring ring ring* of the Salvation Army Santa getting softer and softer, that gold bell chime, receding into the distance, the last refrains of "Silent Night" getting caught in the tree branches, falling down to the ground, into the snow and now nothing but *crunch crunch crunch* under her feet. Beige winter snow boots, jeans and a parka, light blue sweater, scarf, mittens, and a wool ski hat. You had to know how to dress for winter. You'd underestimate it, always, each fall, forgetting in summer what cold meant, what cold was. But you'd make that mistake only once.

The sidewalk in little pebbles and chalk slab, packed-down snow, tiny bits of trees, pinecones, little tiny red things, some kind of miniature berry on a branch, embedded in the snow. Now the Main Street silent, a never-was fantasyland back far away behind the pines.

Through the spindly black bare elms and maples, the *crunch crunch* sidewalk leading Beth down the path to that oyster-colored house falling into itself. That joke of a house, poor Shauna. You had to admit, she got a raw deal. That non-home and that no-show mom and that slumping dad. In a way, it was a miracle Shauna was what she was. Strong, confident, sassing-off half the time, making everyone nervous, bending the world to her will, caving the conversation in. That girl was a survivor.

The suede boots would make it better. Not all better, to be sure. But, at least, something. Something to say "I see you. I see you, Shauna Boggs. We're in it together."

A single light in a square from the kitchen, orange. The pitch-black pines holding up the house. Christ, that meant he was home. Not good. Maybe if she just left the present on the stoop. But she couldn't, right? No way. One-hundred-dollar black suede boots in a gift box with a burgundy bow on a front stoop, no one's looking. Well, you might as well write a note, "Come and get it, fuckers."

She had no choice. She'd have to knock and he'd have to answer, a perfunctory front-step fog of a conversation. Alright. No big whoop. She'd just leave off the present and that would be that. It's not like she'd have to hug the guy.

Crunching up the *creak creak* stairs, raising her knuckle-mittens to the door, she had a thought, a fleeting thought of the wall falling in and there being nothing behind it. A sound-stage. A Hollywood set, nothing more. But before she could finish the thought, before her knuckles reached the door, the door opened and there he was. Troy Trash Boggs.

She hadn't knocked, how could she? Or did she? Forgetting herself, her mind still on the soundstage, Beth found herself standing there frazzled, shaking there in the snow. She didn't remember shaking, didn't remember being cold. But now, suddenly, she was shivering. Shuddering there on the porch, holding her big bright burgundy-bow gift.

"Hello, Mr. Boggs. Um. I brought this for Shauna. It's a surprise. I was . . . I guess I thought it'd be funny to put it under the tree and keep her guessing."

Troy Boggs standing there, moving back. Moving into his house gesturing in. A hitch, there in his walk. A mini-stumble back.

"Oh, yeah. Come on in."

Stepping inside, looking around for the Christmas tree, make it quick, Beth realizes there is no tree. Of course. No Christmas tree in this house.

"It's just. We. Well, we haven't gotten around to it. Just haven't had the time."

Haven't had the time! Yeah, right. All you have is fucking time, Troy Boggs, everybody knows that. What, you have an appointment at two with a Mr. Jack Daniel's, is that it? Johnny Walker at three? Jim Beam promptly at four? A full fucking schedule you have, Mr. Boggs. Don't be late.

"Oh, oh, well, yeah, the holidays are kind of hectic. We just put ours up, actually."

That's a lie. That tree in the Krause household goes up every November, day after Thanksgiving, at ten. You could practically set the atomic clock by the Krause Christmas tree. Dotsy's up at dawn with the tinsel, icicles, lights, stockings, matching Mr. and Mrs. Claus salt and pepper shakers, mistletoe, three wise men, poinsettias, nativity, pinecones, all of it coming out of the red plastic storage boxes, marked on the side with masking tape and a Sharpie. X-MAS DECORATIONS.

Oh, yes, the Krauses sure had time for Christmas. A tree in the living room, a green Douglas fir, and one in the den, silver, for variety. Silver with blue lights, crystal bobbles. A cool-palate frosted tree with icicles and glass ornaments. Maybe we should give them one of our trees? A fleeting thought, but not a bad thought. Beth was pondering. I mean, it is Christmas, after all. What's more in the Christmas spirit than giving away a tree?

Beth was imagining it, how would she do it? How would she ask for it? Would Dotsy be mad? Maybe she'd be proud of her . . . ? She resolved, yes, we will give them a tree. To go with the boots. It's the right thing to do.

"You want something to drink? We got eggnog, left over. Shauna got it."

Still giving the tree to the Boggs house. Not hearing.

"Oh. Oh, no, I couldn't. I should be going. It's gonna snow soon, so . . . "

"Aw, c'mon! Just one drink! For Christmas."

Not wanting to seem rude. Not wanting to come off as better than.

"Okay, maybe some eggnog. Just one, of course. You know . . . snow's coming up."

"No, I know. Here . . . "

Scurrying around to the kitchen, cupboards clacking, *clack, clack, clack.* Troy Boggs coming up with two mismatched mugs. One from Walter's Tackle & Bait. One from Klucky's, down on Third. Presenting each mug on the brown-top card table with a flourish.

"Here you go. One for you. And one for me. Cheers. Merry Christmas."

"Merry Christmas."

Clinking mugs with Mr. Boggs, smiling up. Well, why not Merry Christmas. Why not? He was a human being, after all, flesh and blood, fellow mankind and all that stuff you were supposed to care about. This was supposed to be the season for breaking bread and clinking glasses and smiling jolly.

And now Troy Boggs is in a good mood. The good mood pouring down his throat in warm brown brandy mixed with egg-nog. Not so much eggnog, but she didn't need to know that.

She was quite a looker, you have to admit. This saucer-eyed friend of his daughter with her white-blond mop of hair and ice-crystal eyes. Christ, you could just look at her for days, couldn't you?

Sitting down in his chair, sipping fast on his good mood, maintaining his good mood for Christmas. Christmas spirit. Christmas spirits. Brandy, rum, bourbon. The spirit of the season.

"You know . . . " Shaking his head, smiling, magnanimous. "You just, you just keep getting better and better-looking every year, you know that?

And something in Beth shifting. Something crossing her legs in front of her.

"I mean. What's your secret? I know! It's Oil of Olay. Oil of Olay! HA-HA!"

Clapping his hands together, hard. Snap! Oh, this is gonna be good. His good mood getting bigger and redder and warmer, his good mood clapping his hands hard and slapping Beth on the shoulder, big-hearted.

"THAT must be your secret! Is that it, HUNH?"

Not a funny joke, but meant to be a funny joke. Laugh now, Beth, laugh now at the unfunny joke. Smile at least.

"May I use your bathroom, Mr. Boggs?"

"Call me Troy!"

"Um, Troy, I'm just . . . it was a long walk over and—"

"Oh, no problem! Of course! Mi house is tu house!"

Make your way fast to the bathroom, scurry in, lock the door. A white-and-yellow linoleum floor, yellow-stained wallpaper, coming off at the corners, coming off near the ground, grout peeling. Jesus, how long since they washed this place? Mildew smell. Piss smell. Rust rings around the drain. Lime faucet, hoary glaucous chalk.

Beth wanting to click her heels and be home. Get me the hell out of here. Feeling suddenly caved-in, caught, claustrophobic. Quick pee and get out of here. Don't touch anything, don't touch anything in this place. No toilet paper. Of course. Why would there be toilet paper? Who would buy it? Christ, what a shit-basket.

Wishing she could adopt Shauna, get her out of here.

As she comes out of the mold bathroom, Mr. Boggs is moving fast. Moving fast but what for? From where? What happened?

"Mr. Boggs?"

"Uh-huh?"

"Are you . . . sorry, I just. Is everything okay?"

Nervous now. Mr. Boggs quiet now, staring at the floorboards. Not wanting to say it. Not knowing how to say it. Mister, what the fuck were you just doing? What the fuck are you up to?

"You know, I got something for you! Hold on!"

Now the dark mood has gone away and the good mood is back. The good mood is taking him up the stairs and the floorboards up above are *squeak squeak squeaking.*

And downstairs Beth, looking around, setting the present on the table, nice, a presentation, and poking around, inspecting, trying to figure it out. The walls, the sink, the table, the fridge, the eggnog, the painting.

The painting.

There's something weird about the painting. It's a print of sunflowers on a brown background in a brown lacquer frame. But that's not it.

See, the thing is, about the painting, is that it's off. It's off and there's dust behind it in a rectangle. There's a dust outline but the painting is off, off its dust outline, misplaced.

Upstairs the floorboards creak.

Moving, pulled, toward the dust outline, toward the sunflower print, pulled on a string. Beth did not want to see it. She did not want to see it but couldn't stop the string from pull pull pulling her forward, dragging her forward into the face of that painting, the fate of those flowers.

Upstairs the boards go *creak creak creak.*

You can stand in front of that sunflower painting. You can stand there forever but you don't have much time. You can take your light blue mittens up to the wall, shaking, careful, careful, don't disturb the dust. You can pull the painting off sideways. Shh. Shh. Shh. Don't let him hear. Shush. Keep it down. He could come down anytime. Make it quick. Hurry!

You could take the bright yellow sunflower painting off the nail on the wall. Shh. Keep it down. You could see something there. You could see a spot there, behind the painting. You could hold the painting, trembling, and you could lean into the spot. You could lean into the spot and look through the spot.

You could look through the tiny little hidden spot and see something on the other side. A looking glass! A looking spot! You could look through to the other side and see a yellow-mildew bathroom with yellow-and-white wallpaper, linoleum tile, and no toilet paper.

But the place you would be looking at, the place you would be aimed through from the looking spot, would be the toilet. You could look from the looking spot to someone on the toilet. Someone, say, like you, who was just on the toilet. You could be looking at you. Like Troy Trash Boggs was just looking at you.

Back up now, slow, listen for the squeaking. Put the print back now, hurry, put it back, don't mess up the dust, back up now. Back up! Step step step out the door, step back now, Beth, don't let him hear now, step back now, Beth, don't fucking say anything just get the hell out.

It's funny how, coming down the stairs, coming down in his

good mood, piled high with old dresses, left-back dresses, now presents, present-dresses, he would give to her, it's funny how Troy Boggs was thinking about how these dresses would for sure fit Beth and maybe even she'd try them on, for him, you know, to show him. In the spirit of Christmas.

THREE

Before Jeff. January 1976. Blah winter blank-canvas days. She tried not to think of it. What was the point? Nobody had to know about it. About those things she did. It wasn't like anyone knew, not even miss Goody Two-shoes. If no one knew, it didn't happen, right?

She could've called this guy a client. I guess. Shauna didn't like to. No, they weren't clients. They were friends. Friends she'd met at Dreamers. Friends she'd met at the Jewel Box. Friends she'd met at Captain Jack's. Tall friends. Short friends. Old friends. Older friends. Balding friends. Rich friends. Married friends. Lonely friends. Just friends. Only friends.

Meeting them, sometimes at home. Or, if they were married, the Baymont Inn off Harvey Road, the Howard Johnson on 28th, the one with Holly's Back Door Bar & Grill. One guy, a dentist, wanted her to meet him at his office, on the weekend. A Saturday appointment, four o'clock.

He told her over the phone to get ready, he "had a big one." I get it. Act impressed.

The dentist office a study in beige and putty. Not too many kids' posters around. She'd thought there'd be kids' things

everywhere when she pictured it. She'd thought she'd be looking up at a happy happy tooth-cartoon declaring his passion,
"Don't forget to floss!" But, no, no jolly tooth-advice here. Only
putty-colored tile, putty-colored counters, taupe reclining chairs.

Outside, the oatmeal sky in blotches, little bits of leaves
smashed in the snow-sludge ground, she'd have to peel them off
her boot. Shauna had an outfit she liked to wear to these little
appointments. She'd seen it in *Bonnie and Clyde* last year. A full
wool skirt in brown-black check, a maroon pullover, angora, and,
the kicker, a pair of knee-high black suede boots, a present from little miss perfect. A Faye Dunaway shoot-'em-up getup. Sometimes
she'd even wear a hat, a kind of berry wool beret tilted slightly to
the side. A costume. A costume for a part she was playing. And
this was a part. No question. This was not her. She was nowhere
to be found.

This was her character, in this heather wool outlaw outfit, her
character doing these things . . . walking up the steps, knocking
on the glass-frosted doors, waiting outside in the 4 PM drizzle, the
last light fading through the trees.

This was her character, pretending to be pleasantly surprised to meet the new friend, the dentist, a thin-hair in khakis,
as memorable as cement. Her character, smiling, demure, and
stepping inside this empty bland beige office, walking down the
hallways, being led into a room with a dentist's chair, reclined,
at the ready. She wondered if it'd been left that way or he had
adjusted it back.

This was her character, leaning back in the dentist's chair,
pulling up her plaid wool skirt, spreading her boots apart and

looking like all this was the best thing in the world ever, best-kept secret, best Saturday afternoon, most-wanted kiss.

This was her character, letting him kiss her, letting him grope her, letting him remark stupid guy words about his too-big dick, his monster cock. (Yeah, right, it was just average, but that's not part of the scene, those lines aren't written here.)

This was her character, making those noises, acting like she couldn't get enough of his oh-so-big dick and letting him grunt grunt grunt and fuck fuck fuck her not-there body.

This was her character, letting him gasp and goop and spasm, this stupid-face dentist, all over her belly and lay on top and get up and put everything back together and say some stupid thing, some ice-breaker non-joke, and laugh an embarrassed laugh and hand her six twenties.

This was her character, taking the six twenties, counting them out and looking up at the cement-face nothing-man dentist, telling him, "I thought we'd said two hundred. That's what we'd talked about. On the phone."

This was her character, freezing her face in a pleasant, never-there smile and taking the six twenties after the fuckface dentist, buttoning up his khakis, tucked in his shirt and said, "That's all I have. And anyways, I thought you'd be better looking."

FOUR

Now. Ever since Jeff. Now, that she had Jeff. Now, that she had to keep Jeff.

These union workers coming into town, thank fucking God. They might as well have had a ticker-tape parade. Like soldiers coming back from war, they had saved her.

He had saved her.

It was a ritual she had every morning. Well, it started in the morning and then she thought maybe another one in the afternoon, just to be safe. And now, lately, she'd added a third, at night. All bases covered. Three times, each day, every day without fail, even Sundays.

If he knew, she'd be mortified. But he would never know now, would he? It's just a piece of writing, a note she'd grabbed off his desk, a shirt left at her house, and a couple of locks of hair . . . these were more difficult to get . . . but Shauna Boggs got what she wanted.

Put them down, the note, the shirt, the lock of hair. Seal it in an envelope tight. Write his name, Jeff Cody, in loving, flowering cursive on the side. Light a candle, shut the lights. And pray.

"Dear God, Dear God, please make Jeff Cody love me more

than anything else in the world make him think about me day and night, night and day, make him lust after me, want to fuck my brains out, until it kills him, make him madly, passionately, deeply, crazily in love with me."

Shauna Boggs would repeat this over and over, ceaselessly, fearfully, desperately until she reached a pitch of exhaustion and then, spent, she would snuff out the candle, keel over on the ground, stare at the ceiling, and think of him. Their wedding, the next time he would see her, the last time he saw her, the things he'd done to her, the things he would do to her. She couldn't wait.

Her very heart and soul a sudden frenzy, a panic passion, almost too much for her paste body. Ceaseless. A pacing, ranting, pining, coursing through her head, her heart, the deepest bottom of her belly, between her legs.

All she is, all she ever was, began and ended with him. No more was she the sad little case, the left-for-dead dad's daughter, the welfare girl, the secret child-bride of her father, the wronged piece of meat.

No, no, now she was Jeff Cody's girl. Soon-to-be wife. Maybe. Whatever happened, she would be his. She couldn't fly in front of the bullet quick enough. Oh I love you! I love love love you!

The daggers stabbing through her heart. More prayers! Just this once! Light the candle. Maybe I'll add a fourth prayer a day. Yes! Four is better than three!

Away from him, reaching for him. Always reaching for him, the space never close enough. Jealous of anything near him. Jealous of the buttons on his shirt. Jealous of the cigarette that gets to be between his lips. Jealous of his shirtsleeves. Jealous of his pockets. Jealous of the sheets underneath his chest. Jealous of his pillow. Lucky, lucky pillow. And when he sighs his last sigh, and grins his last grin, she'll be jealous of the box he's buried in.

FIVE

What a party! That late, late summer, dog days, that sticky August heat—even the trees are sweating. The hackberry trees growing out of the limestone, the other side of the quarry like a cliff. Underneath, the water a pine-green blue. An abandoned inner tube bobbing up and down near the sand.

Yeah, so, it's not Malibu, Jeff thought, but who the hell cares . . . everyone is here. There's Shauna over there, Billy and the boys. Skinny rodent Billy with those ghost eyes and rat-brown hair. And what about over there, even little miss Goody Two-shoes Beth Krause came. Look at that, who does she think she is, wearing that white bikini? A string bikini! I bet you ten bucks her folks don't know she got that suit.

Well, cut-off jeans and a halter for Shauna, lusty, available— hair like she slept on it. Yes, she's been spending nights with me alright. Looks like she's been fucked thirty ways 'til sundown with her peach-fuzz skin and her flushed rosy cheeks and her easy, oh so easy, laughter. I made her that. I did that. Pabst Blue Ribbon in a can, might as well be diamonds.

This quarry is a no-no and that's what makes it fun. That chain-link got torn down last June, grass swallowing it now. They say it's dangerous, but it's easy to dive. All you gotta do is push out enough, off the jetty, and you'll clear the rocks below. Don't be scared. We've done it a million times.

Billy and the boys been here since ten. These guys know how to drink. "Union reps." That's a laugh, all that's been repped since we blazed into town is low tongues and lower morals. Billy with his face stoned off. Perpetual. And the pills. And the beer. And the lines, always, cut-up white razor runways. Rampant. Union reps. That's a good one. From all over descended, swooped in, in concert shirts and jeans. Billy, from Ohio. Russ, from Waco. Terrance, from Pittsburgh. Randy, from Detroit, Cass Corridor. Rough place. They knew each other, these guys. You just cross paths on these gigs. Factory workers in town, need some extra muscle, something about overtime, wages. Who cares anymore? You wouldn't think these guys would represent anything—looking like that—except maybe beer in a can and no shirt.

They got Kiss playing on the radio. Leave the car doors open and blast it.

"I-I wanna rock-and-roll all ni-i-ight . . . and party ev-er-y day!

"I-I wanna rock-and-roll all ni-i-ight . . . "

You can sing along, too, if you want. No one'll notice. These bastards are loose, and getting looser. Look at Billy! He's pretending to fall off the jetty! Look at Russ! He's pretending to push him! Oh, yeah, Shauna is not wearing much. They're asking, who's the new girl? The girl in the white bikini. Yeah, her. Man. Oh man. I could show her a few things . . .

Shauna is showing Beth how to jump off the levee. It's better if you take a running start. See. Now Shauna is running and flying off the cement, out off into the air and over the rocks. A sprawl into the hot-glare sky. She made it!

Now it's Beth's turn. Don't be nervous. Show her where to start.

"See. Just go from here, take off and just go for it. Don't slow down. Whatever you do."

Beth looks up, now she's a saucer-eyed baby girl, but tuck her hair behind her ear. Make her soft. Melt her.

"You can do it. I know you can."

That plate face looking up. Eyes like an alien.

"Hey. I know!"

An idea now, running back to the green Plymouth, fast-forward the cassette.

"Just hold on. One second."

Pause.

"Okay, now. Here it comes . . . "

Blasting out of the Plymouth, turn that dial up. Crank it up!

"Beth, I hear you calling

"But I won't be home right now

"Me and the boys . . . "

What a hoot! They're all gonna sing now. Everybody loves Beth (the song) and now everybody loves Beth (the girl). Go, Beth, go! Jump off the levee! You can do it! They're playing your song!

And Beth takes her mark, salutes, takes a running start and flies off the levee. *SPLASH!* Down below into the green murk water.

Applause. Whistles. Hoots.

The sun blazing white through the trees.

Here she comes now, out of the water. Look at her. She takes a bow. Ha. That's a good one. That's a real good one in the white string bikini. White string bikini see-through wet, see-through now, see-through nipples.

Oh man, I could show her a few things . . .

The fall is coming down fast, the trees smelling of wet smoke, summer folding up and then poof gone and just the circus of holidays, marching forward grandly down the road. Halloween, Thanksgiving, Christmas, New Year's. A collective upheaval. An imminent madness, finally a frenzy, a panic, and then the great shriek of New Year's and back to square one.

A four-month ritual from light to carnival to gracious thanks, to beating each other up at the mall to a squeal and a kiss under a tinsel cone hat after FIVE-FOUR-THREE-TWO-ONE! And then, what is it . . . what comes next?

But Shauna couldn't care less about that now, staring at Jeff Cody's back, now sleeping and turned away. A colt. A buck. Her own personal Wild Bill Hickok, Buffalo Bill Cody. How lucky she was. Covered in sweat she'll never want to wash off. Never, never! It's his! It's a part of him!

Trying not to think of the growing frequency between phone calls and the eyes looking around mid-sentence and the fact that he always, always slept with his back turned away.

At the foot of the bed, a window, a window she had looked up at, alone, not all the time, not every night, not like she was stalking him or anything, it's just. Well, he hadn't called. She'd thought he would call and then he hadn't and she found herself, there, right outside there on the sidewalk, looking up. Is he there? Is the light on? It looks like the light's on in the hallway maybe? Is that him? Does he see me? Wait, is that someone else? No, please God don't be someone else. Oh, no, it's him. It's him! Make sure he doesn't see. Did he see me?

Looking now from the inside, from the bed, at that window, how could she be so silly? Of course he loved her. Of course he did. Listen, he fucked her. He fucked her almost every night. And you know what else? He would get shit-faced, obliterated, and confess he was in love with her, grabbing her by the wrists, almost a plea . . . and even though his eyes were rolling back in his head, and even though he kept bumping into the furniture, and even though he was on enough pills to kill an elephant; pills to go up, pills to go down, pills to go any which way around, even so . . . it was obvious he loved her. In vino veritas. It was at this time, these stumbling times, that he revealed himself, his true self, wrapped away and sealed in concrete at all other times. He was a man, you know.

And there's the proof, too. What about that day? Last summer, in Greensborough, they'd gone to El Compadre, a kitschy, cantina-style place with a mariachi band, yellow pepper lights, and margarita specials first Tuesdays. But this was a Wednesday, empty, except for those two secretaries drinking zinfandel. That night, Shauna's head swimming in strawberry blended margarita number three, or maybe four, make it a double. Seeing, and not seeing, the oxford shirt in the next booth. Looks like he keeps looking. Looks like he keeps looking at her.

Shauna Boggs who'd been fucked all day, fucked and then fucked again by Jeff Cody, not to mention then again in the Plymouth right before. Right there! Shauna for once in her life glowing, not to mention that macramé dress, a cream dress, see-through in places. Demure places. Strategic places. And yes, oh yes, the levee tan, the yarn-dress, the summer-fuck-it skin. Forget it. Shauna Boggs was the belle of El Compadre, Greensborough, Michigan.

And then the guy in the next booth, that Shirt with the ruddy face and maybe he's here after work. Red booth, red candles, ruddy face . . . red, red, red and now Jeff Cody is gonna see red, too. Two pills in and three Cadillac margaritas. He is starting to notice. He's starting to piece together the plot here against him and his girl at this here hacienda and there's gonna be a showdown. No, caballeros, two pills in and drink three and he's got a bone to pick, see.

There's a waiter there, fawning. Why is he fawning? Talking to the Shirt about the Mark Cross leather interior of his white convertible Pontiac Grand Ville '76. Now the waiter whistles, says that's one cherry of a car, a real beaut.

Shauna isn't pretending not to listen. Oh, she's listening. Over Jeff's shoulder now. Forget about Jeff. Jeff who? And then the Shirt is looking over. She's thinking maybe he's got something, something Jeff doesn't have. And never will. She's thinking maybe he's got something that makes things easy. Maybe all her troubles will be over, Lord, all that rent and all the white unmarked letters coming in these days, always from someplace in Delaware, all those credit card guys calling, threatening, calling again. And what's she supposed to do with those credit card guys ringing and ringing some more, endless ringing, shut the fuck up. She only has so many hours in a day, so many hours in a night, so many nights of the week. And one of those nights, or two or three, are nights she's gotta spend with Jeff, to keep him, to keep him interested, right? But, lookit, those are nights she's not making money. It's not like she's a prostitute, it's nothing like that, it's just those guys help her out, those guys help her get by a little, right, and Jeff Cody doesn't do jack shit. Nope. Not one cent.

But this guy, this Shirt, well, he could help her out. Big time. And he knows it, too, you can tell because he's looking right at her, right through her, and he might as well just say it out loud.

"C'mon. Lose the loser. I'll make a decent woman out of you."

The mariachi band is singing "Besame Mucho." That Shirt is practically singing it to Shauna, swooning, serenading, smirking, so obvious it makes her blush. Don't let Jeff see.

But it's too late.

It's too late now, Shauna.

And now that mariachi band is no longer playing "Besame Mucho." That mariachi band is playing . . . well, they're not playing anything . . . because they're short one guitar and that's because they got two mariachis standing, set back, staying out of it, and one mariachi staring at his guitar, which was just in his hands but is not in his hands anymore, where'd it go? Oh there it is, that guitar, that guitar going up down, up down, the trajectory of a battle-axe, over and over again, *smash smash smash*, into the head, neck, back, ears, face of Mr. Looky-loo Shirt from the booth next to Shauna. On the floor next to Shauna. On the tile next to Shauna.

Yellow tile grout now gets to be red, that button-down shirt now gets to be red, that macramé dress now gets to be red *splat splat splat*. And the guitar, well, you can forget about the guitar now, amigo. That guitar now in splinters and slivers and splices of blood-splotch wood. That guitar now just a stem, just the neck of the guitar, nothing more. Throw it away.

But that's not all 'cause Jeff Cody's got the Shirt by the collar and now he's dragging the Shirt out, past the mariachis, past the zinfandel secretaries, past the *baños, damas y caballeros,* past the kitchen and the busboys in white. Everybody froze, on a dime, don't turn on us, don't see us, don't look.

And now Jeff Cody drags that Shirt to that cherry of a beaut, that white convertible Pontiac Grand Ville '76, staring straight back at him with its top down, baring its teeth. Dare you to stare down those headlights and don't forget to notice those white-walled tires.

But now Jeff Cody's got a plan to make that interior red, too, and he's got that Shirt and now you can forget about that Mark Cross leather interior, you can forget about those white-walled tires 'cause everything's getting painted red red red. And the Shirt can barely lift his head, but Jeff has him propped up now, propped up now in the driver's seat, it's your car, right.

Shauna's standing there now from the doorway, helpless.

"You like this car? You like this car?! Wanna ride around in this car, huh?!"

And now Jeff Cody's holding the Shirt, squeezing his head against the steering wheel, embedding his cheeks into the metal, white Mark Cross leather steel.

"You wanna take my girl for a ride, is that it? You gonna take my girl on a date?"

And getting quiet now, quiet down into his ears, a whisper.

"See. Nobody makes a fool of me. Nobody."

But the Shirt's got his eyes closed. Pleading.

And then, to Shauna.

"Get in. Get in. I wanna see you go for a ride. I wanna see you on your big date!"

And Shauna standing in the doorway, thinking and not thinking, who to call, what to do, how to play it.

But he's marching to her now, "I told you I wanna see it. I wanna see you on your date! Let's see the happy couple."

He's got her now, dragging her by the back of the neck like an alley cat, over oil stains, over puddles into that white convertible Pontiac Grand Ville '76. He's got her now, setting her down in the passenger seat, next to the Shirt made of blood-splat. That Shirt can't even look up, head on the steering wheel, lolling. The two of them, a zombie couple, shivering, a Halloween funhouse ride.

"Oh, now, don't you look pretty on your date? That is a handsome couple. Yessir."

Shauna looking up from the passenger seat, shaking, "Please, just . . . "

"You want out?" Act surprised, make it light.

Shauna nodding in millimeters.

"Oh, you want out?"

"Yes, please."

"Who you wanna be with? You wanna be with him? He got what you want?!"

"No."

"No, what?"

"No, I wanna be with you."

"What?"

"I wanna be with you."

He makes her hold it. He keeps her sunk.

"Now, that's better."

And the door gets unhinged and Shauna gets pulled out beside him, tucked under his arm and away from that Pontiac Grand Ville '76, driver pummeled dumb at the wheel. You can see them now, strolling soft down the sidewalk, his arm wrapped around her like a dove.

And that is love.

SEVEN

Wandering around unfocused, in the wayward hours between choir practice and her shift . . . making her way aimlessly from the Hackley Public Library, past the Port City Victorian, past the Dockers Fish House & Lounge and finally, inevitably, ending at the lighthouse.

The two red lighthouses, the Muskegon South Pier Light and the Muskegon South Breakwater Light, squaring off. Facing each other like pawns in a chess game.

What did it mean? Her head shook with the possibility. That lighthouse, bright red, in summer, picture-perfect red, white, and blue for the Fourth. The sand of the lake, a crisp white. The sky, a happy blue. The lighthouse, a shining red. A star-spangled landscape, pert as punch.

Then fall, the chill coming in. The trees, burnt burgundy and amber. The lake, a pitch-pine green. The sky, a bruised plum covered in dust.

Then, the blanket of winter wraps itself around the bluffs. All is white. A blinding, barren terrain. White the snow. White the lake. White the sky. But then even the lighthouse contributes. Red! Red amidst all that white. A happy surprise. A tip of the hat to Christmas. A Joyeux Noel. An each-winter present, as recurring and disarming as a Christmas tree.

But always facing off. These two lighthouses. What was the fight? What was the contest? The issue? The conceit? Or was it simply a nothing thing. A trifle. A shrug. Pebbles on the sidewalk. Grass through the cracks, repeating again, "Don't look at me, I'm nothing. I'm not here." As insignificant as sawdust.

And the thought comes to her, almost to focus . . . what it is . . . what it means after all . . . but before it can form itself into a crystal, there's a noise from behind, and it's gone for eternity.

Walking walking out out out toward the water, Beth thinks about all the things she will one day have. She will surround herself with little glass figurines, a fireplace. Molding and a great big imposing colonial-style house with columns and soldier-ghosts and history, history, in every plank of the floor. She will give her daughter her blue Wedgwood locket, the one her mother gave her. History.

She will have a husband with sandy brown hair, a kind-eyed working man. A professional. He will come home with his oxford shirt, sleeves rolled up, tired from the day. He will sit down on the navy-blue wing-back chair and she will coax him back to happiness with a few kind words and his favorite apple crumble. She will kiss the back of his neck and he will reach back and touch her arm, reassuring. I am here. We are here. We are in it together. We are blessed.

Turning just before the lighthouse, a hurried sound of an engine. Beth looks out at the purple dimming sky, purple dim street, hard to tell apart. Thinking for a moment she saw a dark green car, a forest-green Plymouth. But no. That's Jeff's car. And Jeff would be with Shauna. Of course he would.

EIGHT

"It'll be fun, I promise."

"I don't know."

"C'mon. Just try it. Just this once."

Shauna Boggs would've died if she thought anyone would ever see these. It was a mistake. She had put them away meticulously. First, she had put them in the dresser drawer, then under the bed, then in a shoebox in the closet. Which is where Beth found them.

Beth had been over, even though, guilty, she avoided that wooden oyster box of a house as much as was possible without arousing suspicion. Why would she want to go over there? Would you? Walking in there was nearly a seven-in-nine chance you'd stumble on her pop staring into his glass in the kitchen. Hunched over himself at that card table, use-it-for-a-kitchen-table, staring intently into a brown plastic glass of something orange with what's left of ice melted in it. For hours.

She wondered how someone could sit for hours like that, not a word. She would die of boredom. But no, there he was—it didn't matter what day it was, what hour. It was his job and he took it seriously. What was he looking for in that brown plastic glass, opaque, from the Buffy's Buffet down on Henbert. Had to be he stole it. Habit, I guess, to stare into the same glass each morning, each noon, each twilight? That's my glass. My drinking glass! Don't touch it.

No, Beth steered away, delicately, from this little mess of a home, barely hanging on. She had nearly run out of excuses but this time she'd thought what the fuck. Choir practice had been canceled so what else was she gonna do 'til her shift. Besides, Shauna's house was near to work. It didn't make sense to go back home.

They'd been trying on shoes. Then, next thing you know, dresses, this necklace, that skirt, 'til the whole afternoon was burned down and in the hurry of try-on-this and hey-let's-swap a box had tipped over, a little gray shoebox, at the back of the closet and the pictures had come flying out.

Naughty pictures. Dirty things. Sinful pictures her mother would've never allowed her to see, make-her-say-three-Hail-Marys-just-for-looking pictures. Polaroids. There. In the white frame, wide at the bottom, the little black pieces reveal themselves. Shauna in her swimsuit. Shauna in her bra. Shauna in nothing at all.

Shauna on her back. Shauna smiling, drunk. Shauna with a flirty look on her face, spread your legs a little wider, thata girl.

Beth couldn't bear to look at them, but she couldn't look away. Who was this girl? Her friend? Her best friend? In the pictures, now a star. A vixen. A killer of hearts. You would think that what was boiling up in Beth was disgust, shock, judgment, but that's not what it was at all—to her surprise, more shocking than even the pictures, it was envy.

"Jeff took 'em."

All that time, from cradle to hopscotch, from recess to four square, from corsages to prom to graduation to work, to endless days of drab . . . there had not been one, not one time in a single lifetime Beth had ever felt anything other than the obvious fact. She was her superior. Shauna was never as thin, or as demure, or as delicate in her features, as Beth. Beth was the prize. Shauna was the seconds.

Every time, each and every time, they'd met a boy, or a new set of boys, at school, after school, at the roller rink, Beth had stepped back . . . as she was taught, as she'd inherited. Naturally shy, it wasn't that difficult. What would she have said anyway? What was she supposed to say? The patter, the general swamp of facts exchanged between people who knew nothing of each other confused Beth. It was a mystery. A lackluster one. She wanted nothing to do with it.

But Shauna, oh Shauna had a lot to say. Miles! On and on she would go, asking questions, smiling, laughing, teasing, swatting, guffawing. She was a master of this vacuum-language, as eloquent at drivel-speech as a person could get. Beth sat in wonder, at times wide-eyed, at Shauna's ability to dazzle, razzle, and retain. She had to admit, it was a gift. The gift of gab, isn't that what they called it?

Yes, that's what Shauna had. In spades. In hearts! In diamonds! On and on, she'd go every time, and it was only a matter of time 'til the eyes, or the two sets of eyes, in front of her, would move from the face making noises at them to the smaller, more petite, more dainty little face behind her. And this face, this frozen, cautious face would inevitably, cryingly always prove more interesting.

That part, Beth counted on.

How complicated she would seem, just for this saying-void. The less she did, the more wild they became, in their mistaken knowledge, the fury of her had-to-be-profound thoughts, inner workings, desires. Who is this sweet almost chaste but perhaps dirty, maybe dark, maybe brilliant, maybe wise little shy enthralling creature?! And all of this while Shauna prattled on.

So now this.

These pictures, these x-rated filthy things. In one, the one Beth is holding, peering down, unable to let go, Shauna is lying back on a towel, maybe on the lake? But there must've been no one around . . . she's pulled her shirt up, just enough. She smiles a swoony, mischievous smile and the sun makes her dirt hair gold.

Jealous!

Beth had never been envious her whole life. Not from an abundance of confidence but from a sworn-in, do-your-duty belief that envy was, after all, one of the seven cardinal sins and it just wasn't done. That indulgence, not meant for anyone with the last name Krause. Jealousy was a tonic for small minds, an exorbitance of the weak, the devil's work. Both Dorothy and Lt. Colonel Charles had taught her well to stay away from such lily-minded vanities.

It's a sin, dear. It goes against God. It's an insult to all you've had, all you've been given. There's a reason they call it the green-eyed monster.

And so, with this sudden envy, this sudden desire to be someone, Beth didn't hesitate when her best friend since grade school Shauna Boggs took out her Polaroid and told her to lift up her shirt.

Beth was glad to be back at choir practice. Here she knew the rules. In her white sweater set, under the white wood rafters: This is who she was. This here. Not like yesterday. That wasn't her.

She didn't know what had happened. It had happened so fast. Why had she been so weak? Drinking a beer, fooling around. It was supposed to be play. Afternoon playtime, before work. Not what it was.

"Dona Nobis Pacem."

The song they sang nearly every other week. A round. A beautiful round. The soprano part, by far more interesting. Soaring. The alto part, a dirge. She could sing both parts, if someone fell ill, she would step in, knowing both parts by heart. Yes, she was the favorite.

What had Shauna meant by all this? Swooping around, drinking a beer, taking pictures. She'd just meant it as a joke, for God's sake. But here it happened. Not a joke. A mean little trap, somehow, but Beth could not say how.

Shauna had waited 'til Beth was nearly blacked out, rolling back, lazy arms and eyes. She'd closed her eyes and, as in a dream, she'd opened them and known she was not supposed to. Shauna's mouth, her lips, her tongue, on her chest, her bare chest! It was a trap! Beware!

Yes, it was a trap. But she hadn't stopped her. Why hadn't she? What was it in her that played dead, lay back, and watched this maybe-lifelong woozy dream come true? Was Shauna in love with her? Why had she done these things?

Wasn't it a sin to do these things? Licking, touching, kissing, that was for husbands on wedding nights, not girl people in the light of day. One of them a spider, one a fly. But Beth knew, also, she hadn't stopped her. Not what she was doing at first and not what she did later. No, she hadn't stopped that either. If Shauna wanted to get drunk and devour her whole, who was she to stop her? Just this once.

But there was an uneasy thought, a devil thought, coming up from her ears, tightening her throat. For a second, she thought she'd heard the sound of something, something else. *Click. Click. Click.* More taking pictures. *Click.* Wait. *Click.* But how could Shauna have been taking pictures when her hands, her mouth, her eyes were all on her?

Don't let devil thoughts get you. Don't let devil thoughts get you in church.

TEN

The second-story room at the Green Mill Inn was nothing to write home about. Paneled walls, blue carpet, a perfunctory picture of a boat on Lake Michigan, a print of an oil by a mediocre artist. There's a lighthouse but it could be any lighthouse. Dirt blue, beech, and cream.

Room 202.

An even-numbered room, which annoyed Jeff. He didn't trust even numbers. Always he would try for room 107, room 111, room 115. But 202. No good could come of it.

"Did you give it to him?"

"Who?"

"Billy! Did you give him the pictures?"

Jeff keeping her at bay. What a little piece of sausage Shauna was! Packed into her tank top and blue-jean shorts. Those pudding legs pale as Pringles. A lifetime of cornflakes and white bread and beer. Her mouse hair, wet around her temples, yes, they had been up to something. Up to no good. Again. Afternoon delight. Although the afternoons were becoming less and less delightful. She was not the one he wanted.

From that day she had paraded him around like a pink pony

in the front office, it had pulled him back like a tide. Drawn him to and fro. In and out. Crashing again and again into the impossibility of it. She was too good for him. Shauna, ha—well that was easy. But Beth. No. She would take work. And even then.

"Listen, ya can't tell Billy you know about the pictures, okay?"

"I know, I know. Geez."

"It's just guy stuff. That's all."

That phone call he'd gotten, so sudden in the middle of the afternoon. "I'm here with Beth and we're taking dirty pictures. Billy would die!"

Yes. Billy. That's what he'd made up. A stupid little trifle of a lie. To cover. "Why you asking so many questions about Beth? You in love with her or something?" And it just slipped out. "No, fuck no . . . Billy thinks she's cute is all."

Since then, a weird obsession, an overzealous engagement on Shauna's part. "Tell Billy." Or "Yeah, Beth's coming. Get Billy." Or "Maybe Beth will be there . . . hmmm . . . maybe ask Billy, huh?" Such a stupid little child-girl fantasy she'd put together. The importance of it somehow magnified, he could not imagine why. So he'd played along. "Ha, oh yes" and "Oh, I will." Wink, wink. And he'd played along, sure, he'd played along that afternoon when got that phone call.

"Billy would die!"

"Wait, what?"

"Beth's over and we're taking Polaroids. Billy would freak out!"

He could not say how or in what state he'd managed to fling himself over into that little situation. All he knew, hearing her words, was that he had to get involved.

"I'll be right there."

"Yeah, you guys should come over. Pretend it's a surprise."

"Yeah, okay."

Why the fuck would he call Billy? Let's be plain, Billy didn't even know who Beth was. It was all made up, for Christ's sake. But there she was, Shauna, going on and on about it.

And now, these bad-girl pictures. What the fuck was he supposed to do but stare at them all day. Over and over. Then put 'em back. Forget about them. But then, again, bubbling up, boiling over, get them back again. Stare stare stare at that lily-white little miss perfect Beth Krause and think long and hard, strategize, how to get her.

Shauna prodding again. "You know, I think Billy'd like Beth."

"What?"

"Billy. He'd like her. Don't you think?"

"Listen, I wouldn't set these guys up with a dog, let alone a girl. They're thugs, Shauna. Half these guys are ex-cons."

"But I thought you said—"

"Yeah, right. Unions aren't what they used to be. It's payola. Half of it's greased. More than half."

"Yeah, but Billy's nice. Quiet kind of."

"Shauna, he's done time, get it?"

But she's not listening. Tricks and setups. Knowing more than the next guy. This is the sound of wheels turning.

The ivory-sand beach of Lake Michigan, the red dusty clouds, billowing in the distance. Red sky at night, sailor's delight. Red sky at morning, sailor's warning. Here, now, the dusk over the picket-fence in the sand. The brush in the dunes. The slate-gray water today, almost still. Lap lap lap from across the lake, all the way from Canada, those waves!

Lap lap lap, a lullaby lull Beth leaned into. Lingering on the sand, skimming her hands over the twisting fence, daydreaming the day down the shore, the lighthouse in the distance. One day she would have a fence of her own, not a wind-worn falling thing but a white picket fence, a dream fence and behind it a dream house. A white colonial with black wood shutters. A rose garden. Maybe in the back, a trellis. On Sundays, she'd have Mom over and they'd drink tea and talk about the garden. A lovely storybook, small but graceful life she would quietly steer through the morass, the chaos, the darkness.

As calm and true and gracious as her mother, as strong as her father through Normandy, she would prevail.

Behind her, emerging from the trees, a figure, not her friend. Shauna had asked her to come here but that wasn't Shauna, was it?

She had never looked at Jeff, really. Other than to note his height, his dark hair, dark eyes. That was all. An assessment. Seeing him now, his features coming into place, she hadn't realized how desperate his eyes, as if he startled even himself.

"Beth. Don't be scared. It's just me. Jeff. Remember?"

"Why should I be scared?"

If she hadn't been before, she certainly was well on her way now, having set it in her mind.

"Shauna's running late. She sent me to tell you."

"Oh . . . okay. Thanks."

Turning toward the shore, that was the end of it. Something about this Jeff from out west disturbed her. He was full of himself. He seemed a construction of billboards and cigarette commercials—but talking to him, taking in the stumbling blocks of his thoughts, there was nothing there. A thin veneer of interest. Yes, he looked more than attractive, dreamy even, to someone like Shauna. Someone dying to be dying of love. But get past a few subjects, you'll see. He's all hat and no horse.

"Beth. Um. Beth, I was wondering if you . . . were cold. You can have my jacket."

Staring out onto the blue-charcoal water, she hardly heard him. Yet heard something. Turning, she saw him closer. Now. Too close.

"It's okay . . . Jeff." She struggled for his name. "You don't have to wait with me."

Please go away. Go away! I don't want you here! What do you want from me?! Jesus.

But now Jeff was closer.

"Look, Beth. I just wanted to tell you . . . "

"What?"

Searching for something to say, anything.

"My friend, um. My friend Billy. He really thinks you're something."

"Oh."

What a fucking grunt. Who the fuck is Billy? The wind getting cold across the lake. She'd had enough.

"Look, will you tell Shauna to just call me, my shift starts in half an hour, I don't have all day."

It wasn't what Jeff had meant to do. Meant to say. He was making a fool of himself. Him! Jeff Cody! Goddamn this girl really drove him off. That was it.

He grabbed her and pulled her to him. Fucking little doll face, don't you see?

"That's a lie. I made it up. It's just. Beth. I was supposed to leave two weeks ago. I was supposed to leave two weeks ago to go back home and I can't leave, I can't go anywhere, I can't do anything or get anything done or walk and talk and think because of . . . um, because of you."

Silence.

Lap lap lap from the shore.

And then Beth, soft as the breeze through the reeds, "Are you making fun of me?"

"What? No! No, are you kidding?"

"I think I'd better go—"

"Beth. Look at me."

And Beth looking down at the sand. There was a castle once. A vague memory of a sand castle with four turrets, a tower, and even a moat.

TWELVE

In that moment between dreaming and waking, that moment before all the myriad little nothings of life come flooding, cutting you off, killing you—there he would be, Jeff Cody, in her almost dreams, semiconscious, pulling her, pulling her toward him.

To want, to want not to want. An endless enterprise of grasping away from him, away from him, must get away. But always the moon pulling the tide, back back *lap lap lap*, back to him.

That first night, how clever! How he'd taken her to the Swingline factory, the lights in a buzzing glow, the machines sleeping, the gears at rest. A funny little secret moment between her and Jeff and the machines. No one will know. The echoes of the metal casings, *clink clink clink*. The clock, every clock, *tick tock* at the center, up up high, lording over the factory, lording over them, doling it out.

How many times had that clock been looked at, been pleaded, oh, please, pleeeease, go faster, please get done. Life awaits! But no, the clock answered, this is your life. Face it.

Jeff Cody walking behind her, watching her taking it in. A sigh to it.

"I read in *Newsweek* in twenty years this won't be here. None of it." Beth staring at the ceiling, a vent three feet wide crawling down from the rafters.

"C'mon."

"No, that's what they said. No more factories. They said it'd be like a ghost town."

"Yeah, right."

A girl-shrug. Look, she'd read it. It wasn't her fault.

"Where'd they go? Huh? What'd *Newsweek* say about that?"

"I dunno. China."

"Ha! See what I mean. They don't know jack."

She stops now, contemplating the line of time cards. Punching in. The clock. Don't forget. Punch in. Punch out. Don't forget to punch out. You'll get docked. One minute late is fifteen minutes late, don't forget it.

"Buncha Chinks don't know nothin' about making cars. Get serious."

The light ending at this side of the factory. Lights out. Lights on. The break room to the left. The mini-fridge, just like at the Green Mill Inn. Beth thought there would be something in that mini-fridge, something left, something gross. There always was.

Two-month-old sour cream. Leftover hoagies. Takeout.

Those mini-fridges always a lesson in sadness, a lesson in neglect, a lesson in who-gives-a-shit-anyway. Just leave it.

"Kinda makes me sad."

"What?"

"That article kinda made me feel like . . . I dunno . . . like we were losing, like we were gonna lose somehow."

"Oh, sugar."

And now his arms are out. His arms are out and around her, pulling her, pulling her in.

"They don't know shit. That's just some dumb reporter gotta make a deadline."

Hope. There is hope after all. Beth's face letting it take over, open up, open up. The clouds do part. The sun does shine. We will win!

And now she is pulled in and he is wrapped around, a Brawny paper towel affection, somewhere deep in the morning hours before light and the coming of the dreaded Chinese. They would never win. They would always be less. We would never be shamed.

Taking her head in his hands, little doll head, come to me. He would kiss her on that little button nose and say, "I'm gonna take you out of this one-horse town."

A sort of smile up. A scared sort of smile.

"You watch."

And nothing more. Not a kiss. Not an advance. A statement. He takes her hand. Little hand, follow me, and walks her out of the factory, out away from metal sleeping and lights buzzing and clocks *tick-ticking* away. Time is running out.

Then the next time. The second date. A mystery. . . He takes her out to the levee, now in winter. She'd never been. He closes her eyes and leads her over the snow, through the sugar maple woods, a crystal cathedral of dangling branches and, hidden away, at the end of the path, an ice rink, the water frozen two feet thick, the same water that in summer had enveloped her white bikini body now a slab of stone, a flutter of white marble, but that's not the best part. Hold on. Hold on. Keep your eyes closed. Now! Now open.

And Beth opens her eyes and now the ice pond is lit up. A million little white lights in the trees. Christmas lights. He'd strung 'em. Look, there, he plugged them in. Some kind of mini-generator, a box that makes light, and now the levee. . . .

Beth looking up, the crystal ice chandelier, the twinkle branch overhang like nothing ever before, this effort, this beauty, the beauty of the effort, this man who'd do anything. This man in love. Or was it love? Maybe it was a trick. Maybe some kind of joke. She couldn't make sense of it. The whole thing, overwhelming. Like pouring an ocean into a teacup.

And now this man coming closer, a hesitation. A puzzle.

"Wait. Why are you crying?"

And it's true, Beth standing there, not one but two tears, one for each cheek, a crystal drop, water made of quartz.

"It's . . . it's . . . so beautiful. . . . "

"Oh, darlin'. You're so strange! How 'bout that? I build you a lit-up ice rink and you start crying. Jesus, there's no hope!"

"No, no, it's just . . . I've never seen anything like it."

"Well, you better get used to it. I got lots of things to show you. You just wait."

And now, handing her ice skates. "See I got 'em. Hope they fit." He puts down a blanket, too, sets her down on the rocks. I'll help you. One at a time, each skate. Hard to lace up in this cold, hands shaking.

Beth quiet now, watching him knelt down before her. What did it mean? What did he mean? What did he want from her? I mean, it's obvious. She knew. But he got that everywhere. He got that from Shauna and, for all she knew, he was still getting it.

"Jeff ..."

"Uhm?"

"Does Shauna know about us? I mean, does she know, you know, that ..."

"Us?"

"Yeah, you know."

"What us?"

"I dunno. That we're here."

"Is there an us?"

"I dunno."

"Do you want there to be? Maybe?"

But Beth doesn't answer.

And now the laces are finished. Done. And now Jeff Cody stands up tiny Beth Krause on her feet and escorts her to the side of the ice. Careful. Careful. And now he sets her free.

"Go on now. Let's see what you can do."

And Beth now in the middle of the ice cathedral, the branches leaning in trying to grab her, hold her, hold that beautiful thing. The zillion-light twinkle and Beth in the middle, skating grace in her ice skates and white fluff ear muffs. My little angel, he thought. How will I get her? How will I keep her?

Jeff Cody wanting to put a giant glass casing over them. Stay. Stay. Stay here in this glass gleaming case. Stay here in this moment forever. Don't leave me.

And then the third date.

A shudder.

The third much ado he had made. Sitting there in the White Swan Inn Bed and Breakfast. She'd told her parents she was spending the night with Shauna, a dangerous lie, she knew. But they would never check. She knew that, too. Shauna, to them, something they didn't need to see, something they didn't want to think about.

The B and B a historical monument. The best bluegill in town. The restaurant below, the best on the lake, it was said. Better than Mes Amis. A jarring thing, at dinner. The waiter had poured the wine and he had made a joke. A dumb joke. But it was embarrassing, the whole setup. The purposefulness of it all. Beth felt overwhelmed.

"I just . . . This is all so . . . Impressive." Not wanting to hurt his feelings.

And Jeff raising his glass. *Clink. Clink.* Now they drink their Santa Cristina Chianti 1973. And he sets down his glass.

"Darlin', everything I do is to get to fuck you."

The audacity! The vulgarity! The vulgarity of the audacity! Beth almost spitting out her wine, not knowing what to say, what to think. Profane profane profane against elegance elegance elegance. Christ, did anybody hear?

He smiles now, a sheepish grin. "Just being honest."

And this silver-tongued devil before her, this Jeff Cody from God knows where and God knows who, she would leave him. She would get up and walk out. She would throw her drink in his face. She would slap him.

And maybe that would be something she would tell Shauna.

"I told you he was bad. Just a fucker." She and Shauna would laugh and giggle. She and Shauna would share a snicker at his expense. They would tear him apart!

Except, Beth sitting there, across from Jeff Cody, who had just said that don't-say-it thing, had just happened to, yes maybe, just happened to fall in love.

The first snow of 1977! Look at it! Little soapsuds fall fall fall from the blind white sky. She wanted to share it. Oh, why wasn't anyone here to see? Mrs. Krause had said Beth was out and Jeff never answered his phone these days, never came round unannounced like he used to. But the first snow of winter, well he'd come out for that, surely.

The trees were made of crystal now. Winter wonderland trees. Ice and white and fluff fluff snow. A fairy tale. Maybe Beth could come out and they could be stupid. Build a snowman, make snow angels. It wasn't that far, she could walk it bundled up.

Huddled and running through the picture-book trees, she thought for the first time in years of her mother, who had left her. Why had she left? This snow maybe. This cold, spare, shutout life. This non-success. Watching the day die down, day after day, why would she stay? Why would anyone stay? And it's true. Nobody did.

Or if they did, they were cursed somehow . . . cast under a spell that makes you stare in a glass all day, hunch over, look into it, watch the ice cubes *clink clink clink*. You are getting sleepy. You are getting older. You are getting sunk. Read your future in the ice cubes. Nothing there.

Ice on the tree branches! Ice on the trunks! A magic glass world. Everyone inside, the streets a set with no players. A scene waiting to be played.

That too-American ranch house with a flag, always a flag—except at night. You have to take the flag down at sundown, out of respect. And Lt. Colonel Krause did so, of course, like clockwork. Shauna hit in the stomach each time she thought of the vast ocean of difference between the Lt. Colonel and her own shit-sack of a dad. Why had she been so unlucky? And Beth gets Mr. and Mrs. Perfect over here in their perfect American ranch-style house with their perfect flag and perfect lawn. You'd never see the Lt. Colonel hunched over a glass at noon.

Sneaking into the back, she'd done it a million times—taught Beth how to sneak out, too. Just shimmy out the window, grab the sill, and plop down. Make sure they think you're in bed now, fast asleep. The back of the house, the linoleum floor, the staging area for proper things up front. The great room, they called it. No, there certainly wasn't a great room in Shauna's house. Not even a mediocre room.

She had seen the blueprints, once, going through the attic with Beth. Here's the kitchen, the dining, the nook for breakfast, and the great room, with a fireplace, won't that be nice in winter?

But the fireplace wasn't lit and the house was empty. Shauna stepped back to look at the molding, the wallpaper, the china cabinet . . . everything in its place. Everything just so. How different her life would've been had she been given such propriety, such concord, such grace. Who knows what kind of elegant form she might've cut. A lady.

In the other room, a sound suddenly. Muffled, a strange sort of shock of a sound. A gasp. An inhale. Maybe something in pain. Tiptoeing through the hallway, past the black-and-white pictures, parlor-style, it grew louder, a hiccup, almost a whisper. The empty-house secret in another room. Peering through the almost-shut door, there a strange figure. A wild figure. Something in trouble. A confusion of arms and legs spread wide.

A girl, yes, a girl lying flat on her back—next to her, on his side . . . a boy. Yes, that is a boy. They are staring at each other, staring into each other's eyes, a magic-spell stare from another dimension. Unearthly. Divine. But not just any boy and any girl. A girl named Beth and a boy named Jeff Cody.

Flying out of the hall, backward, grabbing this way and that, grabbing something blue and white, a cameo, not-thinking never-thinking, bat-wings and stumbling, knocking the pictures off the walls. And then over the linoleum. Get me out! And back into the snow. Running running out through the fuck-you picture-book landscape, the crystal trees, the magic glass forest not hers anymore.

This is not for you.

This is for them.

This is for the people in love. Not low-rent hookers with daddy-boyfriends and doughnut thighs. This happy white winter world is a stage, but you are not a player. You are maybe an extra, really a stagehand. No, no, this is for them. The lovers. The two in love. Deeply in love—did you see his face? Did you see how he looked at her?

Was that the bang-bang, look-away, sweat-and-go way he

fucked you? That dog-sweat, use-you-up fucking you'd so longed for, dreamt about, missed?

Those dark villain eyes of his staring in that magic-spell at her? These trees made of glass their paradise. Not yours. Not yours.

How could you have been so stupid to think anyone could love a fat whore like you.

Coming out of the snow, like two branch hands, these two trees, buried up to the wrists. One open, reaching up toward the sky, the other clenched, sinking into itself, closed. Between them a bench, empty, staring out on the lake. Waiting for its victim. A white-gray day, snow on the ground, making a glove on the trees, gray sky, gray air, gray lake.

It was Thanksgiving Day and he knew he wasn't invited. Didn't even ask. No, they would never let him in. Not him, Jeff Cody, the son of a salesman, a traveling man, and now he traveled, too.

Those build-up years from Topeka to St. Charles to Ames, rambling down the road next to his dad in his suit, selling vitamins, selling Bibles, selling vacuum cleaners, you name it. The movies getting color and Marilyn Monroe. How simple and grand, expanding it was. America! Progress! Coca-Cola! And all the building, an embarrassment of appliances, a toaster oven, an automatic shoe shiner, look at this knife sharpener for your wife. It had seemed the whole decade had been sponsored by GE.

Going to see *Some Like It Hot* in the theater in Tulsa, a fairy tale he'd begged his dad for for weeks. And when Pop said he was going for some popcorn, maybe a soda, he didn't even take his eyes off the screen. Thirty-foot Marilyn Monroe in that white shimmer dress, coochi-coo, that baby voice, that platinum hair, those lips, that mole, taking it in as a boy, hypnotized. So transfixed, so feverish it was impossible to remember what his dad had said exactly, something about popcorn and when he'd be back. So spellbound that even as the theater spilled out and still no sign of Dad, he'd sauntered out in a trance, giddy with Marilyn, mad with too-young lust, where to put it? And even as the lights get turned off, the projectionist scurries by, the box office closes, and the teenager behind the concession stand closes up shop—looking his way. Hey, kid, you alright? Even then it didn't hit him, couldn't hit him, that Pop wasn't getting popcorn and wasn't in the theater and wasn't coming back.

Tulsa it is! For a boy not yet seven with no folks and no money, a foster life of cots and oatmeal and midnight stealing. A bout at Cedars, then Sacred Cross, then a family from Plano down in Texas took him in. Almost. They met with him. They met with him four times, actually. They showed him pictures of his new home. A split-level house. In the back, a swimming pool with a diving board and all. He picked out a new bedspread. A surprise he would spring on them, to show how easily he would fit in. He would fit in and be part of it. He would contribute. They could count on him.

But, in the end, they'd decided to go with someone younger. A new kid with blond scruff hair, just turned four. Couldn't blame them really. How could they know he'd picked out a bedspread? A crazy thing to do, he told himself. It was his fault. Maybe he'd been too desperate.

He vowed never to be desperate again.

Then, at eighteen, catapulted gloriously, savingly, into the '60s. He'd been a hippie, mostly for the pussy. The drugs suited him. Going from place to place, flying from drug to drug, "hanging out," fucking this girl and then that girl. His long hair a trap. A signifier. I am one of you. I belong.

The first time of his life, belonging, taking part. How heartbreakingly easy, California in summer. How spellbinding the eucalyptus, the ice plants, the bougainvillea, the sun bursting through it like hope itself and acid and mushrooms, what else you got? That seven-year marathon of pot and tripping and "waking up," "tuning in," and "burning out." He wanted it never to end. How rewarded he was for the years on the cot. How vindicated!

And then, stumbling into the '70s, the late '70s a comedown. A slowdown of gears and, finally, the necessity of a job. This union gig was something he fell into, a passing thing. All this organizing, these meetings, it was a natural progression from his wide pant legs and collars. It wasn't political. He wasn't political, never had been. The '60s radicalism was all well and good, but he was in it for the sex and drugs, who wouldn't be.

And the traveling, always traveling, organizing, manufacturing plants in Detroit, and Cleveland, up north to Milwaukee. These were teamster jobs, sturdy business. A jackleg operation. And let's face it, these guys were lowlifes.

Billy and Terrance and Russ, all of 'em. Thugs. But he wasn't a thug. Not him. Of course not. No, no, he was different. He was in love.

Staring out from the bench, under the two trees, out at the gray glass lake. What the fuck could he do to get her to love him back? How to impress her? How to make her look at him like Shauna looked at him, desperate, longing, scared? Poor Shauna. Poor girl. He hadn't meant to throw her under the bus. He really hadn't. It just happened.

"It just happened, Shauna. I fell in love."

He told her quietly, in earnest. Trying to be the man he sees in movies. A sensitive man, rugged but caring. A progressive man, not a dick. He wouldn't like to think of that terror in her eyes, that abandoned frenzy. Why had she put so much on him? Why had she staked her soul on him—a dirtbag, a drifter, what had he to offer her? Can't you see I am broken?! Can't you see I'll tear you apart?!

Why the fuck couldn't Beth look at him like that? With those pulling eyes and pleading neck and lips desperate to kiss, to quench, to suck, parched with loneliness. Why was she always, instead, just out of reach?

Thanksgiving on his own then, facing out toward the *lap lap lap* of the charcoal water on the milk sand shore. He would find a way to make her love him. He would grab her and not let go.

Peas. Pot roast. Potatoes. For dessert blueberry pie. Everything laid out, kind and crisp. The Lt. Colonel, his wife, Dotsy, and their daughter cut into their plates while the storm howls outside the window. Slate-blue-and-cream wallpaper. Ivory tablecloth with a white lace runner. Each of it, all of it, just so.

"This wind ought to build up the shelf ice."

It was often this way with dinner. A few statements of fact from the head of the table. A few nods of assent, maybe a smile. Yes, dear. Bite. Slice. Spear. Nibble. Nod. Bite again. An easy dinner, not much to say, no need to say it.

"Looks like the Packers aren't gonna make the play-offs."

In the adjoining room, the slate-blue sofa, the slate-blue La-Z-Boy aimed at the TV, wood-paneled. The very TV they'd watched the Ice Bowl on ten years earlier. The Ice Bowl. What a game! Ten-year-old Beth and her dad crowded around the television, watching Bart Starr drive down the field in the punishing cold. No whistles. The refs' lips would freeze to the goddamn thing! Yelling out the calls in the forty-below windchill, snow coming down, ice on the field. Figure skating. Down 17–14 with only four minutes left. Goddamn those Cowboys. And not even the band had played. How can you play when the brass section can't even put their lips to their instruments, the woodwinds contract in the cold, useless. Six of them treated for hypothermia after the pregame show. No, please, they can't lose to Dallas, not now. Not here in the freezing cold at Lambeau Field.

But there is Bart Starr calling the Packers' final time-out with sixteen seconds left. One yard to go. Just one yard! The Lt. Colonel and his daughter glued to the TV, unable to breathe, unable to nibble at any of the numerous treats set out by Dorothy from the red-and-white checked Betty Crocker recipe book, Appetizers and Drinks section. All of it green and yellow. Go, Pack, Go!

Sixteen seconds left. Third and goal.

Bart Starr runs off the field, consults with Vince Lombardi. Runs back. What'll he do? Throw it and hope to the good Lord he makes it. Or what about a field goal and we go into overtime? Overtime! In this cold, forty-three below and only getting colder. Snow falling, how can you see?

Sixteen seconds left and father and daughter clutch each other's hands. Oh Lord, please make it!

Sixteen seconds left as Bart Starr runs it into the end zone and the Packers win! The Packers win! He ran it! Can you believe it, he ran the ball!

21–17 Packers!

And the Lt. Colonel and his daughter are jumping around the room on a trampoline, reeling, ecstatic, rapt. Dotsy on the couch laughing, her hand over her mouth. The game of the century, maybe all time. The Ice Bowl. And we were in it together, you and me, Dad.

Later they'd find out Starr had told Lombardi he wanted to run it. And Lombardi had replied, "Well, run it in then and let's get the hell outta here!" Nothing else like Lambeau Field. Nothing else like the Packers. The goddamn mother-loving cheese-heads. Little Elizabeth Krause and her father, all their lives in love with the field of time between October and January. A glorious time. Crackling leaf season. Game after game season. Lazy Saturdays and Sundays spent in front of the TV, fire in the corner, each curled up in a blankets, up to the waist. The Lt. Colonel's chair, the La-Z-Boy, sacred. Only for him. Beth on the sofa, sometimes Dotsy, if she wasn't up to something in the kitchen. Always a new excitement on the stove, in the oven, in the Crock-Pot, slow cooking. sauerbraten, stroganoff, strudel, pot roast, goulash—thick winter stick-to-the-ribs dinners, fit for a fire, next to the tree. A graceful thanks, roast turkey and then all the Christmas decorations taken out and placed, Mr. and Mrs. Claus salt-and-pepper shakers. Poinsettias. Pinecones. Tinsel. The tree. The three wise men. The ornaments. Each thing, each token, a memory.

The stockings embroidered by hand by Dotsy. "Charles"—"Dorothy"—"Elizabeth." Over the fire they hang, as simple and serene as the nativity. A Midwest trinity of quiet, modest, humble means. Our home. No, we are not millionaires, but we are good people. Softly, in gestures.

And Beth liked nothing more than these football Sundays, tucked in by the fire. This was home. Thinking, now, at dinner, the storm outside chopping the lake to pieces. She could never let them know about the bad things she did. They must not know.

Jeff had to be kept far, far away. He made her guilty. He made her do things she knew she wasn't supposed to do. With his dark brown hair and eating eyes, a villain-face, he devoured her.

Wanting not to want. Wanting not to need. Hog-tied. Not seeing herself as the angel atop the tree. Not seeing herself, in fact, at all. Where am I? A glass figure in a glass globe, swirling. Where will it land? The snow frantic, shaking, blind.

Everybody knew the shelf ice was a death trap, widow maker, never-go-there-ever. Everyone knew you couldn't tell, with that blanket of snow above and months and months of the wind whipping down from Canada, where the ice was thick as cement, layers and layers tightly packed, and where it was like a sheet of glass, air pockets seven feet down. You'd go through it and never see daylight again, plunging deep into the freezing black water, you couldn't tell where you fell, no light through that six or seven or eight feet of ice, snow packed on the top. They would find you in spring.

Even so, Shauna Boggs stood feet in the sand of Lake Michigan, moving forward, drawn. Even so she seemed trapped in a death-grab, a call from the lake. This is the only way to stop the sleepless night and stomach-pit and heart falling into itself. This is the only choice. Salvation.

Come.

The white sky and snow and sand almost heaven already, a gateway. Come. Your time is come.

Entranced by the shelf ice in mountains, jagged across the shore, a mini-Alps every winter ooh and aah, taking pictures. The water coffin below.

One foot off the sand, onto the snow would do it. Start the clock. You wouldn't walk far. Everywhere around signs. SHELF ICE—DANGEROUS—KEEP OFF!

Lifting her foot to take the first step, it came to Shauna, dropped down like an ice cube.

No.

I'm not the one who will die here.

He could not get close enough to her, couldn't dig down deep enough under her skin and crawl inside. The thousand unnatural slings and arrows of his youth, somehow erased. By her. Only by her.

It was the cure, the tonic, the medicine he'd never known could exist, all encapsulated in this little pill, this blonde doll-of-a-girl pill, taken once daily, twice daily, never enough. Answer the phone! Come to the door! Look at me.

Jeff Cody. Helpless for this pill. There was no antidote. Withdrawal symptoms: A cold sweat. Panic. Anxiety attacks. Possible seizures. Staring down on her saucer eyes, now closed, the saucers off, her child-girl breath sinking up down up down on her chest. What could he do? What could he do to take her out of this panel-wall Green Mill Inn and with him forever? His panic pill, his medicine, his cure?

He could not lose her. That was simple. Stay with me. Stay with me 'til the moon flies outward and the earth spins fast and the sun grows into a million billion trillion suns and devours the earth and the moon as one. 'Til the end of the green-grass trees, the ocean tides, the days into nights and nights into days. Stay with me 'til the end of the light, the last blast, the last dying days of oblivion. Stay with me as the earth and the moon are enveloped, devoured, scorched by the sun, and you and I shall cease to be as one. I will carry you.

In the morning light off the ice-lake painting, a terror thought, a kill-you thought. What if she left me?

EIGHTEEN

Making his way over to Sanborn's on Henry, his dark green Plymouth flying over the slosh pebble streets, Jeff Cody might as well have been levitating.

This is the day. This is the day he'd do it. Saving up, he'd started not knowing what he was saving up for. Maybe a cruise, maybe a trip out west, maybe even a trip somewhere unheard of, someplace like Bali, Tahiti, Fiji, with bright umbrella drinks, giggling native girls, and inedible insect platters.

Someplace he'd be gone and gone for good, lost forever to this too-planned, over-gridded nation, turning quickly into something he'd not quite understood, turning briskly away from that free-spirit '60s and now, shimmying up to the '80s, what would come?

But now, this winter, this town, this most romantic, exquisite, exotic place on the globe. Muskegon, Michigan, a paradise of delights.

And now, having saved and saved for those stupid, child-boy fantasies, he knew, knew now, that there was only one point, one arrow, one vector for this savings. Beth.

Beth Krause, he would marry her, here, right here in Muskegon at St. John's, maybe even the chapel choir would sing. Maybe even she would sing, sing at her own wedding. Oh, wouldn't that be something? Now, that would be something to write home about. If there were any home to write to.

If there were any parents to take her to. "Ma, this is my girl, Beth and me, we're getting hitched!" And then later, "Dad, the wife and I are comin' down for Thanksgiving, we got news!" And then soon after that, maybe even a baby, a baby boy, a towhead, maybe name him Wyatt.

None of that. No, never. But he didn't need that. Why should he? When he had Beth, both the sickness and the cure. Beth, both the little girl lost and the lusty woman he could bury himself into, each night, every night, for the rest of his boundless days.

She would die when she saw this ring. He had one picked out of the paper. A green-and-white diamond emerald jobby, with the green in the middle, crystal on the sides. An oval-shaped stone, a trio, in silver setting or platinum, couldn't decide.

He would take her hand in his, get down on one knee, maybe at that French place, Mes Amis, down on Main. He'd wait until dessert. Or could he wait? Christ, he'd be so jittery. He couldn't hide it, no, he knew. Better tell her up front, over champagne. A champagne toast! Then, he'd spring it on her.

What if she said no. Impossible. But . . . what if she did? Oh no, he couldn't think about that now. It couldn't be. No, no . . . not after last night falling asleep in her arms, collapsing into her. Not after staring deep into those blue-ice eyes, owl eyes, eyes too big for her face, falling into her. You, you. What have you done to me? What has happened here? The same story, an ancient story, repeated here, again, for the trillionth millionth time. A man falls in love with a woman. Time stops. Never anything before and never anything after. A suspension of season, tide, the thousand natural shocks of past and future disintegrated, dissolved into a dew. Nothing bad. Nothing bad ever again.

The outside of Sanborn's a mirage of twinkling necklaces on dismembered bloodless necks, headless beauties, all in a line. Dress me. Drape me. Destroy me before I destroy you. The brisk stab air nowhere to be felt by this young man, this husky action, moving forward, forward into the store, a ring, a future. As certain as stone.

Inside, an older woman. A Russian. On the phone. A quick look at Jeff and a size-up. Not a sale.

Jeff, seeing himself in the mirror magic sparkle glass. Not a bad-looking guy. Handsome even. Handsome, yes, everyone told him so. All the girls, all the myriad girls. And Shauna. Not quite Beth. Not quite yet. But she would. She was just being shy, you know.

Work boots, a navy parka, light blue jeans ripped at the knees but only a little. What's wrong with him? There's nothing wrong, right? It's just a parka. It's an ice-cold day and he's wearing a parka and hiking boots. What gives?

"Can I help you?"

Russian lady buries the phone in the crook of her neck. Vague bleary words coming out of the receiver. Maybe her husband. Does he own the store? Is this the owner? Is this the owner's wife? Why is she looking at me like that? God, is it that bad? Am I that bad?

"Yeah, I was looking for this ring."

There, take it out. A newspaper clipping, folded, why did it look so pathetic all of a sudden? Yellow, framing red, the emerald ring in the middle over the print. While supplies last! Final sale!

That was just this morning so of course they'd have it. How could they not? And anyway, they just say that, say that to get you into the store. Scam you. It's all a scam, see.

"Sorry, sir. That one's out."

"What? No, you see, it says right here—"

"—Out. We don't have it. Very popular."

Was it his face? Was there something about his face? His hair! Maybe his hair's messed up. Not thinking, his hand up to his tawny hair, combing it down, making it look like a casual gesture, a thinking gesture. Add a sentence.

"You see, it's for my fiancée. Or my future fiancée. I want to ask her. Want to ask her tonight."

"No more left."

"Listen to me!"

And now, the phone gets grasped. The phone gets lowered slowly.

"Sir, I'm going to have to ask you to leave."

"No, listen. Listen, what the fuck? I'm just asking for a god-damn ring! I'm just asking to come in here and BUY a mother-fucking RING like you advertised here in the NEWSPAPER!"

"Sir—"

"I mean, what the fuck? Why PUT a fucking ad if you're gonna treat people like this?! I am a CUSTOMER. A CUSTOMER in your store!"

And now she's speaking Russian, speaking thick-goop words into the phone, words welded together with Vs and Ws. Gobbledygook bad-guy words made of lead. Cold war words. Spy words. Into the phone, getting faster. Hurry.

"What the fuck are you saying? What the fuck are you saying, you fucking old bag? Go back to Moscow, you fucking fat sow. Why don't you fuck Stalin, you fucking borscht-face pig?! Fuck you!"

And her face stays still, stoic-still, Stalin-still. But her hand goes forward and a button is pushed. A button is pushed in Sanborn's on Henry and now an alarm goes *ping ping ping* through Jeff Cody's skin, heart, veins. Get the fuck out of here. Get the fuck out.

And the green Plymouth can start fast and the snow can crunch under the tires and the borscht-mouth can swear in Vs and Ws through the dismembered row of necks. But somehow the ring cannot be bought.

NINETEEN

A rowdy night at Dreamers, full moon and all. A Friday night and something in the air. What will happen? What will happen next?

Sky-blue jeans and a deep-red halter make Shauna the guy-fuck fantasy of the night. And Beth, beside her, boatneck and denim skirt . . . wishing to go home. He isn't here.

While Shauna does shots, plays pool, wracks 'em up, orders another drink. Still . . . he isn't here.

Growing impatient, staring at the clock, trying not to notice the slobbery, herky-jerky souses on every side. Pickled. The black-and-white checkered floor, the red painted walls, the drunken snapshots behind the bar. Piggy faces, Polaroid hollers, obscenities frozen in time. An endless parade of pickle faces teetering cheerfully into obscurity, the past, oblivion.

Beth is not amused. Shauna and her dumb plans.

But there was also the guilt. Shauna had confided in her that Jeff had left her for "another woman." Shauna had cried, wondering who it could possibly be.

Beth couldn't bring herself to tell her.

What was she supposed to say? "Well, Shauna, now that you mention it . . . the other woman is me."

Shauna crying to her for hours, asking repeatedly, "Who could it be? Who is it?!"

And Beth silent.

But tonight Shauna wanted to "forget it all, let it all hang out."

She had to come, she insisted.

"C'mon. It'll be ladies' night! . . . It's ladies' night and the feeling's right . . . "

And Beth relenting, guilty.

Wanting to say no . . . wanting to be only with Jeff, wanting to lie in Jeff's arms, curled up, slow fucking. Jeff. Jeff. Jeff. The pit of her stomach, a constant longing. A constant lack. Nothing makes sense, all is prologue, an endless smattering of pre-show music, the orchestra in the pit warming up, violins, reeds, strings, oboe. Until Jeff, swinging in, the symphony. The aria. The requiem.

And he's not here.

Watching Shauna at the pool table, bending consciously, provocatively, to shoot the orange ball into the corner pocket. Lotta green in between. And the licking of lips. The endless need of hers to be noticed, be the center. Look at me. Men. Look at me! I am here. I exist.

(I exist because you see me.)

Beth slips out into the ladies' room, never meant for a lady. Plum-painted cement with black Sharpie marker, lipstick, pen graffiti. "Amy sucks donkey-dick." "Berry's a fag." "Todd and Mira True Love Always." "For a good time call Carla: 1-800-SLUT-CITY."

There's a stall in the back and toilet paper in wads and ribbons on the ground. Beth waits by the mirror, pausing to catch herself. No, I'm not a rare beauty but I'm not that bad. I can't be. Jeff loves me. I am loved. I am beautiful now.

And here comes Shauna barging into the tiny cleaning-product vomit-girl room of Dreamers. All voice. Leaning in, best friends for sure, teetering sideways, speaking a little too loud.

"Lookit. I gotta talk to you."

The toilet flushing from behind the stall. Out of the stall, skittering, a middle-age frazzled blonde ducks behind them and out the door.

"Beth, I don't want you to get hurt."

In the background, Led Zeppelin screaming the speakers off.

"What are you talking about?"

"Jeff. I'm talking about Jeff. I know it's you, okay? I know about you and Jeff."

"Shauna—"

"I just . . . I think you should know something."

"Look, I don't—"

"I'm still fucking him."

Suddenly the screaming music, far away, slowing down.

"I'm still fucking him, Beth. And I'm not the only one. I just don't want you to get hurt."

Such a stupid kind of concern. A hate concern. A Sunday Baptist picnic concern. A gossip-over-deviled-eggs concern.

"But, hey, you know, what do you expect from a thug, right?"

Beth pushes past, out of this puke Windex plum box.

"You're drunk, Shauna."

"Beth."

And now, a sensitive smile, a look of concern . . . laying her hands on her shoulders gently.

"Beth. He gave me your locket. See. I have proof. He stole it from you and he gave it to me."

And, magically, it appears now, that blue-and-white Wedgwood cameo locket, out of Shauna's hand. Evidence.

"Look. I'm real sorry, Beth. I couldn't believe it myself. I know how much this means to you. I just. Well, I really care about you and I thought you should know. And I wanted to give it back to you. 'Cause we're friends."

The plum box getting smaller, crushing in, the walls of the trash-compactor toy death star. Closing in. Closer. Closer. Closer.

The walls closing in and Beth gulping up for air, seeing herself in the mirror, weak, defeated. Styrofoam trash in the trash compactor toy. Garbage.

Hands, hands, reaching up and over and out onto the lip of the sink. Throwing water on her face. Awake! Alert! Not a victim. Not a patsy. I'm no one's fool. I'm not a fool. Tearing off her sweater, letting down her hair. Now she's a girl with tousled hair in a flimsy white tank. Pinching her cheeks, she turns to her too-tall friend.

I need a drink.

Forgetting made easy, by the glass. Bottle up and explode, shatter your heart like a sunburst. You can't hurt me now, nothing can hurt me now. I am invincible. Led Zeppelin means I'm invincible. That steel crescendo, crushing time. Building up to me hurting you, I will get you back. See how I get you back. In gestures. Watch me now. I'd like to take this opportunity to show you how it's done. I am trying to break your heart. I'll show you. I'm gonna show you tonight.

Some go softly. I go loud. Hit me again. I'm gonna burn this night to the ground.

Billy's here. He's the one that has it for me. I know what I will do with Billy. I know what I will do. Start slow. Start with laughing. Start with laughing and play swats. Turn this bar inside out. Play swats and giggling. Girl-style revenge, made easy by the glass. I can play pool, too. I can make that corner pocket shot and turn all eyes on me when I set it up, too. Look at me. All of you. Play swat and giggle. I will eat you alive. I will turn you against each other. Who gets me? Who gets me tonight? Wouldn't you like to know, fuckers, fight it out.

Shauna's taking pictures and I don't give a fuck. Look at me now. You don't stand a chance. You made a monster. The room starting to spin now, keep spinning spinning spinning. Let's spin this wonder wheel. Let's see what happens with Led Zeppelin in the background and me on laps, his lap and then his lap and then his. I can do what I want. Watch me now, fast and loose. Revenge made easy, by the glass. Here's how I hurt you back.

How quickly you can tear the night to pieces, stumbling forward into the back room. Dark, sweat-smelly, sticky-floor room with a passed-out drunk on a red puff booth, lining the walls. Beer swill and cigarette smoke drift drift drift with "Sympathy for the Devil" building up from the jukebox. Billy with his ash hair, tumbling down into the booth, yes, now it is coming.

I know how to make revenge in cool blows to the heart at dive bars. Watch this, Billy. Before you know it I am sitting on your lap.

Little girl jokes. "Tell me what you want for Christmas, little girl." Ain't it a gas! What a hoot! I can pull your hand between my legs, under my skirt. Here, in a public place. In a back room with whiskey air and see-through smoke. Here. With that dead man snoring in the corner, belly up, I will show you how bad a good girl gets. Now, you never think I will do this but you never knew me anyway, yeah, that's right, we're in the back room of Dreamers, being bad bad bad but you are in love with this moment and we will kiss and lick and suck but you are not Jeff but we will kiss lick suck this heart to pieces, kick them to the floor and shatter the ground.

All you have to do is not think of Jeff. Not-Jeff. Not-Jeff. Jeff. Not you is who makes me go. Not-Jeff. Not-Jeff. Jeff is what makes me. Jeff doing this. Not-Jeff is the one between my legs now. Not-Jeff trying to burrow into me. Not-Jeff trying to lift my skirt. Not-Jeff thinking it's all a joke. Not-Jeff trying to get me.

Not you! Not you, fuckface!

Get the fuck away from me. Don't touch me. Get off me. No I don't care if you "get off," go fuck yourself. Kicking you off me and leaving you cold, stumbling out the back door, through the parking lot, stumbling home.

Yeah, I left you high and dry, so what? That's how you get to see who I am. Yeah, I'm gone now before you knew what the fuck happened. Now you see me. Now you don't.

The blind light from the road swooshing by. I know, I know, I shouldn't be walking. Teetering home in the dead night, I can make it, it's not that far. Fuck Shauna. Fuck Shauna and her oh-so-earnest "I don't want you to get hurt." Oh, yeah? Isn't that exactly what you want? Stupid cow. Pudding face.

Snow and ice-slush on the ground. I got this one. I got a home and a bed I can get to. I got a car pulling up now. A middle-age fat-bag with an unsteady smile.

"Need a lift? It's awful cold . . . "

Tumbling back a step, taking him in. What would it be to get in a car with an ox of a stranger? Who would I be then? What would that make me?

It doesn't matter now. He's got me. He's got me, heave-ho, and lifting me to the passenger seat.

"We gotta get you someplace warm. Geesh. Your lips are blue."

Who gives a fuck about my lips and someplace warm. There is nothing warm anymore. The front seat, a spinning cage, spinning dash, spinning rooftop, spinning window. Outside the street-lamps looming by like sentinels.

"I just don't want you to get hurt."

Giddy with satisfaction. Giddy with revenge. Giddy with watching it unfold. It's working. I think it's working.

Shauna sits tight. Rifling through, rifling through, watching Jeff from the corner of the room. Dark blue carpet and a wood cork wall. A picture of a lighthouse in a pale beech frame. A seascape.

Soon they would be shipping out to Scranton. All of them. Soon he would be gone. No more Jeff. No more dark hair and swagger and heart-killing nights at Dreamers.

She could make him love her. She could. It was easy. All she had to do was show him these pictures, tell him the story, get a few witnesses—if he needed. No, he wouldn't want anyone to know how deeply it struck.

Leveled.

Jeff, sitting on the far corner of the bed, muffled sheets of teal and peach, staring down at the tiny white squares.

There she is. Pictures in the middle of the white squares. Look at her. Boy, she is really the life of the party, this one. Let them paw you. Let them ogle you. Let them do what they like. My Beth. My little Beth. Elizabeth.

Not mine.

Not mine anymore.

Now she belongs to anyone. Now she opens her legs to anyone. Now she hikes up her skirt for anyone. What else does she do?

"I just thought you should know."

A voice from the depths of the sea, not ten feet away, but a world away. A voice rings out of the darkness. Imagine. Coming out of this potato girl. Potato face. Girl made of pudding who I used to fuck. Look at her now. Standing there, earnest, yearning, leaning in, concerned tilted eyes. Professing what? What does this blue-jean girl in the earth-stripe sweater want with me? Why is she here? Why did she come here? Why is she still here?

Go away. Go away, blue jean. Just because I turned you out doesn't mean shit, you hear me. I turned you inside out like I did a million girls, a million times. Do you think I remember their names? I'm a fucking crook, for God's sake. A low-level jackleg crook, no less. Couldn't be more less. Yeah. I fucked you, pudding girl. White thighs. Why are you still here? What do you want from me?

Not enough pills to make it go down, not enough pills to erase it. Jeff swallowing the amber bottle, tipping it back like a shot glass, who the fuck cares, right?

"It's just. Beth is like that. I know. I'm her best friend. . . . She hurts people."

What a crook! "She hurts people." What after-school-special schoolhouse drama is this. "I'm her best friend."

Some best friend.

Showing up here, out of the blue, out of some kind-heart act, with pictures, evidence, of your oh-so-best-friend getting pawed, getting licked, getting off.

Out of the abyss, out of the blue pitch carpet, she's emerged, to spy, to report, to ruin.

"Jeff—"

Without a word pudding-face is pinned to the wall. A-ha! I've got you by the neck. Held up to the wall by your stupid neck, stupid face. I'll fucking kill you right now. I'll fucking strangle you right here at the Green Mill Inn. I will make you pay, you gloppy little piece of shit spy reporter. Shatterer.

Shatter her.

I will shatter her.

No, no, it's not you I want, pig-face. It never was. I want something else now. Something frail and beautiful and betraying. Something I wanted to take with me to Scranton. Something I wanted to marry and move to California and make a home with baby and Mommy and me. Something I would tear my hands on the stars reaching for.

Beth. My little Beth. Elizabeth.

Nobody makes a fool of me. Nobody.

TWENTY-ONE

Waking up in an unknown place. Not knowing where, what happened, why am I here? Staring at the stranger pig on the sofa. A nice place. Made of brick. Wood floors even. An afghan pulled over him, stranger blob snores into the morning.

I woke up here. In this nice room, a bedroom, a boy bedroom. Man bedroom. King bed. Green sheets. Bedding. A design. A thought behind it. He lives here. This is his house. His green bedspread. His things. How did I get here? Waking up in an unknown bed, tucked in the sheets fully dressed, even my shoes. Funny.

Tiptoeing past the stranger and out the side door, through the pantry beige beige beige and out into the white snow blanket. Morning, no clouds now. Just crisp white sun and a bright blue sky, freezing cold, freezing cold bright white light glare off the snow. There's a sidewalk and a street and a diner four blocks down on the corner—look at that OLD MILWAUKEE sign coming out from the brick-lined streets. Not far from the library. I know where we are. I know where I am. Me. I know where I woke up. Not far from the library. There's a diner and I'll call for a cab. Say I spent the night at Shauna's.

Shauna.

What did she tell me last night? What happened? Something about a locket. Something bad.

Just get home. Get home. Get to bed. Crunching across the snow, down the sidewalk, what a miracle it seemed. Morning. A new day. Each time. A new day. A simple majesty.

How gleaming, how full of wonder, how grand.

How lucky. How lucky I am.

The luckiest girl in the world.

TWENTY-TWO

How silly to make night come at 4:30, dipping down into darkness before even the evening news. Sitting in the wood-panel box at the Green Mill Inn, these endless nights of sundown. Never light. Never light. The closing in of sunshine, the caving in of blue. Banishing hope to spring.

Drawing a blueprint of the house she would one day live in, a colonial house who knows where . . . maybe down in Georgia or maybe Santa Barbara, someplace warm and swimmy with palm-tree summer nights and cool pine winters. No snow. Enough of snow.

"Guess what."

Beth looking up from her blueprint, cover it up before she sees, she'll say it's stupid. Standing there in the doorway. Shauna Boggs. A parka and gloves and a flyaway little smile, rouge, and lip gloss. Hair teased.

She hadn't seen Shauna for days now, maybe over a week. Not wanting to see anyone. Not wanting to leave the house.

"Um . . . what?"

"I got a surprise for you."

The clock on the wall behind, above the door, a school clock. 8:30 PM. Gonna be a long night, this one. Bored already, drawing blueprints.

"Oh yeah, what kinda surprise?"

"We got a party to go to. I got you the night off. A birthday party."

"I don't know."

"Look, they said you can just close up. Slow night. And your birthday coming up and all. Anyways, they like you."

"Yeah, right."

"Um, look around you. It ain't exactly Grand Central Station. Call 'em if you want. I don't mind . . . C'mon, it might be fun."

"Well . . . alright, maybe just for an hour or so. I still got some bookkeeping."

"No problem. I think it's just nice if you show up, you know, just say hi."

"Yeah, okay. Where's it at?"

"It's a surprise, silly. I got a blindfold and everything."

"Weirdo."

"C'mon, it's part of the fun."

This is a funny gray house out by Route 31. A shitty little wood-clack thing, seems like only one room from the looks of it. Taking off the blindfold. Tah-dah!

Inside the party's in full swing, blasting Santana from the corner speakers and the girls and guys swimming with beer swill and cigarette smoke playing it up. Playing the part. Not a bad party but Beth wasn't staying, she knew from the minute they walked in she wasn't staying.

Not bad people, really . . . just not her cup of tea. Okay, a little low maybe. A little too old, too, frankly. Also, no fucking streamers or nothing. No kind of birthday party, for sure. Shauna probably just got a cake and would spring it on her. Some announcement over the music and the obligatory happy birthday, that's it.

Let's just be honest. Not her scene.

"Hey, Shauna, I appreciate this and all, but I kinda feel guilty about leaving. I should go back and clock out at least."

"No sweat. I understand. Let's just go see who's here, say hi, and get back. I invited a bunch of your friends from Hope, maybe they're upstairs."

Rolling her eyes, not wanting to be here anymore. Not wanting to think about Shauna inviting her old college friends, here of all places. This dump. She would have to explain . . .

"See lookit. They're playing your song. Right, Superstar?"

That black circle drop-down and the needle pointing. The Carpenters now, up through the rafters. Karen Carpenter, with a voice like glass.

Up the rickety-rick stairs and to the landing on the right, a murmur of voices coming through the light, smoke.

Into the room and now something's changed.

"Take a good look."

The door shut behind her and now something nervous, sinister through the rafters. Look around the room and there is Billy, there is Russ, there is Terrance, there is Randy. Not a single schoolmate. Something's wrong. Something's rocky and warbled, greedy eyes and in the corner, tied to the beam, a rope. And now there's Jeff Cody. Step out like the star. The ringleader. His circus.

The song from downstairs softer now, muffled.

Shauna turns, what role is this, what is happening, or is it happening at all?

"Happy birthday."

If this were happening, which it's not happening, can't be happening, but if it were happening, there would be here a knock on the head, a dull clock, and then a thud. You would see and hear twenty cuckoo birds like an old-fashioned Looney Tune you watched with your dad back home. If this were happening, but of course it can't be happening, you would be thrown down in the corner on the floorboard planks and before you know it you would be pinned down by God knows who or what but there would be nothing you could do. A circus game called the Jawbreaker, take a ride, buy a ticket.

Those lulling lyrics drifting up the staircase.

If this were not what it is, which is a dream, a nightmare dream that of course you will wake up from, in a cold sweat and look around the pin-quiet room, the safety of home, and sigh and thank God it was all a dream, if this were not a dream it would be you, now, kicking and screaming but now there's something in your mouth and now there's something covering your eyes. A blindfold. Tah-dah! What kind of dream is this—a circus with the ringleader, step right up, ride the Tilt-a-Whirl, now the Gravitron, now the Zipper. The ringleader, your Jeff Cody—the one who begged to come to Thanksgiving and begged, pleaded, to take you away with him. Come away with me.

The tiny song, somehow a lullaby.

What strange dream is this with Billy and Russ and Randy

and Shauna, too, yes, Shauna, too, her voice from the corner. In this dream she is doing something strange, she is riding the Screamin' Swing, but no it couldn't be that she's yelling, it couldn't be that she's shouting, it couldn't be that she's egging them on? In this dream that's not happening she is rabid she is feral she is saying things like that'll-show-her and yeah-that's-right and take-her-down-a-peg. Now the Jump N Smile, now the Crazy Wave, now the Rocket Ride, but they would never say you deserve this, they would never laugh and say that, they would never say ha ha now you know don't fuck with us, little miss perfect.

And now the song, a prayer.

If this were happening, which thank God it could never be, because there could never be a party, a real live party, with folks downstairs smoking and laughing and guzzling it up while upstairs there's a girl not yet twenty-three and hog-tied and everyone yelling a three-ring ordeal, a Ferris wheel, getting kicked getting sliced getting diced, a knife show, a knife-throwing show, and these things could never happen 'cause if they could then what would be the point of storming the beaches of Normandy, what would be the point of praying to Jesus, what would be the point of singing the soprano part of "Ave Maria," if these things could be happening?

The tiny song makes itself tinier.

Oh no, what sort of strange dream is this with Jeff Cody, circus master, he is wearing gloves, why is he wearing gloves? Jeff Cody who said sweet nonsense and future promises and love love love, he would never hurt you, could never hurt you. He would die before he hurt you so now you know it's a dream. In a dream you can never die. Did you know that?

The voice like glass, extinguished.

In a dream you can never experience your own death. See? Have you ever? No. No one has. So, that, too, is a sign that this is obviously a dream, logically a dream. And this is not, this is not, this is not really happening. No, you see Jeff would never hurt you and now you know, with his hand around your throat, playing Tumble Bug, playing Topple Tower, playing Pinwheel, his hands now both around your throat, his hands digging in further, the cameo locket, blue-and-white Wedgwood locket, you'll give it one day to your baby girl, no, he would not, could not. You can't die in your dreams, remember? You can't die before that colonial-style house maybe on the middle of the coast somewhere maybe someplace quiet you can't die in your dreams, remember that. It's impossible. He could never. He would never ever. He could never, ever hurt you.

TWENTY-THREE

How many different kinds of silence can there be? Staring at the ocean, a big blue silence, the vastness of the universe, what does it mean? Standing next to your one true love, your reason for living, a long deep red pulling silence. Love me back. Oh please, love me back. Driving in the car at four in the morning, Jeff, Shauna, and Billy, a body in the back . . . a charcoal silence, as fixed as ash.

What will become of us? What have we done? Did we do this? Is this happening? What happened? How did this happen? How did this happen so fast? If so . . . if it is so . . . what does it make me? Who am I now?

I am not who I thought I was.

But then, who am I? Who is this new person I inhabit? A killer. I am a killer.

Driving through the 4 AM snow, wanting to dim the headlights. Wanting to scream. Wanting to unwind the clock. Make the hands move backward. Stop this watch, for God's sake! Stop it, stop it now, before someone gets hurt. But there is already someone hurt, someone hurt in the back. In the trunk, someone so hurt in fact her eyes are made of glass and she's staring at me.

She's staring at me through the trunk. Oh Lord, make her stop. But the Lord is not listening. No, no. He will never be listening again. He has lost me. He has left me behind. Or I have left him. I left him when I walked into that tricking room, that grabbing house. Left him for good.

Two headlights peering into the pitch black, making two blare cones of light. Nothing else on earth, only us. Erase us. Erase us.

Jeff coulda let them do more, they wanted to do more, boy, did they. But that was the line. Even as she bled buckets, bled white, he put a stop to it. Flabbergasting, the logic. Something male and owning.

Please God, don't let anyone see us, don't let anyone notice us. That's all we need.

And now Jeff will not speak to me, has not spoken to me since the house, didn't want me to come. Grunted. But he isn't speaking to Billy either. This silence is generous.

Up ahead, headlights in the crossroads. Please God, don't be a cop. Out at four in the morning, maybe someone else coming home from a party? Maybe someone else ducking down, ducking from the cops? Oh Lord, that's a Crown Vic with a black door. Oh please fucking God. Oh fuck, God, it's a cop. Now the light is red and the cop is coming toward us. The white-and-black cop car is coming toward us and it's gonna pull us over and that will be that, jail for life, a body in the back, for God fucking sake. A body in the back! There's no way out of that one. That is sent down for life, right there.

But the car turns left. Holy shit. Turns left. Away from us. Away from us. We are saved. We are safe. For the moment. Better keep moving, keep moving for miles, add on, add on distance, keep moving for miles through the black blanket night.

Pulling up to the ditch on Route 31. No cars, no sound, no light. The tires on the snow the only sound, a rolling crunch, a destination fulfilled.

And now the car, at a stop. This is it. Now is the time. If I bite my lip I can take it. No one tells me to stay in the car. No one tells me to get out of the car. I am not here. I am nothing again.

In the front, the two doors open and quick, a task, they are out, slamming the door shut, a kiss-off. A stay-put declaration.

Now goes the trunk. Open behind me. I know what's inside. I made what's inside. There they go by the side of the car, each taking an end, each with a face made of iron. This is not me doing this. You cannot see me doing this. With my face like this I am in disguise. Not me. Never me.

And now, far away from the light, where will it be? Where to put it? What makes the decision? Maybe crucial? Maybe this is where we slip up. Maybe this part is the great mistake.

Getting out of the car now into the ice-pick cold, walking through the flutter flutter snow. There they are, the air in huffs in front of them, talking. Words making vapor. Whisper air. Keep it secret.

"No, don't fix her dress."

"What th—"

"They'll know we knew her. Fixing her dress is a tip-off."

Ignoring me still. There she stares, in the bone-white snow under the sharp-teeth trees, black spindle hands reaching out. Take her. Get her off our hands. Hide her, dear fucking Lord.

Hide these staring eyes, make them stop looking at me. Stop her, she is blaming me. She is trying to take me with her.

Now they are walking back to the car. Again, not a word to me. Again, nothing.

"What about the tracks?" Billy, nervous.

"The snow will cover it, supposed to get worse."

Back to the ash killing house, the lights downstairs dim. But still music, voices. Someone turning down the volume. Shh. A happy happy song. KC and the Sunshine Band. Not much sunshine here. Some sunny place out west, a mockery in the snowdrifts.

"Did they hear us?" Billy, taking out a cigarette, not wanting to go in. Cold air puffs and Pall Mall smoke in a jean jacket.

"No, we're fine. They didn't see."

Won't there be any last words for Shauna? Any final instructions? Maybe an acknowledgment. I am here, Jesus. Something to hold me up. Something to cling to, late night, keep me standing.

"Boggs, you say one word . . . you're next."

A kick in the teeth.

That sallow wooden house on the outskirts of town, two windows above looking down, watching me. You know what you did. We all know what you did. A sapping KC sunshine song, laughter through the snow down in flurries. Snow laughter, giggle snow. But that laughter and that sunshine song not for me. That laughter and that sunshine song never for me again.

PART V

Rich! Who'da thunk it? Jesus, 2003, after all those years of painting houses, drywalling, installing floors for peanuts. Now this. Seventy. Five. Thousand. Dollars. And here, at this place, this manna place, it was just getting better. Mount Pleasant Meadows, Michigan, a heaven place, a dreams-come-true place where you bet ten bucks on the ponies, one hundred bucks back, one hundred on the ponies, one thousand back. This last week alone, Troy Boggs had made five thousand. Five thousand in one week! Oh, what was he thinking? Why hadn't he come sooner?

The world was his oyster, and beside him . . . Terry. Well, she was a stand-up gal. Terry from Clarkston, a TV blonde in a coral shirtdress, sun-wedge shoes, and that sleek, all-over, never-burnt tan. Oh, Terry was something. She sure was. An Oprah disciple. A Regis fan. He was gonna marry her. Maybe next week. Hell. He might as well buy a ring and put it on her finger after this next race. Had to. Can't lose her. Not this one. A real looker. A catch.

Maybe he would even marry her on a day like today, here at Mount Pleasant Meadows. The sky a big bold blue, the eggshell wood promenade, champagne toasts in the clubhouse and everyone in hats. He wasn't looking so bad these days himself, you

know. He'd fixed himself up right. A jacket for days at the ponies.
A jacket and a just-bought hat. Terry noticed him right away. At
the club bar, drinking mint juleps, watching the stakes race. Not
that he hadn't noticed her on the way in. That blonde fuck-me hair,
wasn't that the point, that you would notice, that everyone would
notice, from across the parking lot, the clubhouse, the track? Oh,
sure, she stood out, a real Clarkston belle. Back home, she said, she
grew up on the lake. Sure, she was a step up, a house on Big Lake
and vacations up on Mackinaw Island. But he was her league now.
Her league, with his Seventy. Five. Thousand. Dollars. Pushing
him up, propping him forward into success success success now.
Possibilities, properties, deals. Now was the time. Now was the
time to cash in. Cash in all of it. Maybe buy another house, out on
Pontiac Lake, or Elizabeth, put Terry in the house and never look
back at those dirt dog days on the outskirts of Muskegon.

And, Shauna, what about her? Well, he couldn't take her
with him. That's for sure. An embarrassment, an embarrassment
now. Three hundred pounds! Three hundred pounds of inexplica-
ble moping, dragging around. One-syllable answers and looking
at the ground. Christ, he was ashamed of her. Couldn't even introduce her to Terry. He'd never see Terry again.

And the drinking. Before, a tonic. Now, a celebration. A celebration of life, of the Meadows, of Terry, dinner at Mount Pleasant
Winery, nights at Green Spot. Terry's even introduced him to some
new friends, nice people, classy people. And they were celebrating
too. All the world's a celebration at Mount Pleasant Meadows. All
the world a spinning cycle of who's up, who's down, the jockeys,
the ponies, the stats. Terry's friend, he had a suspicion maybe an

ex, just bought a pony himself. Easy Living. He was sure to be a hit, strong bloodline, clean stud book, lineage back to Byerley Turk. Oh, no . . . Easy Living was just that. Easy Living. And maybe, maybe, if he played his ponies right, Troy Boggs would one day own his own Easy Living, watch his own thoroughbred in the post parade.

He and Terry.

Staying at Terry's. She had a condo. A nice one with sleek lines, a wet bar, and a sunken living room. Everything gray, silver, pearl, and chrome. A slick little hideout with a view of the Meadows. A clubhouse here, too, with a pool table, a ping-pong table, an ice hockey table, an outdoor grill, a common area, a Jacuzzi, an Olympic-size pool, and a battalion of lounge chairs. Oh, it was shared space, of course, with the rest of the association. But, you know, you never saw anybody, never saw a soul out here, really. So it was practically yours.

Terry had been married before, too. Poor dear. Some head honcho at Chrysler, treated her like yesterday's takeout. Some big swinging dick with hair plugs, you can tell from the picture, boinking his secretary after hours, during lunch break, even on weekends for a quickie, while Terry waited at home crying her eyes out, heartless jerk. (One day I'll fuck his shit up.)

Well, she showed him. One lake house, two Chryslers, and one condo later, she showed him. Bastard. And now, Terry was set. Terry was set and he was set and they'd be set together. Easy fucking living is right, assholes.

Meeting Terry's friends in the clubhouse, well, it wasn't easy. But he was a man, sure. He was not a bad-looking man. A man you wanted around. He looked the part. He matched the wallpaper. Yep, he'd do. He'd do for Terry, poor thing, she'd been through a lot.

Gone were the days drinking Coke and gin or whatever was left out of his brown plastic Buffy's Buffet glass, staring at the floor. No how. Not now. Not anymore now with Terry and the ponies and his Seventy. Five. Thousand. Dollars. Nope. This was it. Easy Street.

He knew for a fact, Terry had Two. Hundred. Thousand. Dollars in the bank from her settlement. Not that he'd ever take advantage. No, no. Not him. Terry was the real deal. He woulda run off with her in a pickle-barrel, sure, but with this, well, it didn't hurt. Security.

Spending all day Saturday at the Soaring Eagle Casino & Resort, what a day. Coming down Sunday by the pool, Terry in her peach pants and sweater set. Coral earrings. Unwinding now over white wine spritzers, still warm for September. Still sunny, seventies, not a cloud even.

I mean, yes, sometimes he would hide a bottle or two, but why tell Terry? Sometimes she would fall asleep and he'd have a nightcap, what's wrong with that? It was perfectly normal.

Somewhere in the front office, a buzzer beeping incessantly. *Beeep. Beep. Beeeeep.* Jesus, that thing's been going all morning, what the hell's going on?

Troy sick of it, making his way to the front glass doors, next to the water feature, a wall of waterfall rocks. And there, outside the glass doors and gray stone waterfall . . .

Shauna.

All three hundred pounds of her.

Not wanting to see it. Not wanting to be seen. Oh, fucking Lord. Not here. Don't let Terry see! Hurrying over, hurrying her in. We'll go to the condo. That's it. I'll just take her to the condo. We'll talk in private. Just me and her. Don't let Terry see.

"Dad?"

"Hi, Shauna. Well, what a surprise."

Troy Boggs polite. Troy Boggs in panic.

"Shauna, let's just. How 'bout we talk over here. Good to see you."

Good to see you! Ha, what a laugh. No, Shauna, it is not good to see you, just as it is not good to see yourself. Look at you. Christ. How do you even get around like that? How do you fit in a car? On a seat? In a doorway?

Through the peach-and-turquoise wallpaper hallways, little palm-tree sunsets over ocean water and a gazebo, pretty little sunset scenes, innocuous as mustard. Drywall paradise. Frosted tulip light fixtures, turquoise carpet, Shauna inspecting it all. So this is where you live, huh? This is where you've escaped to?

Brass-frame glass mirrors every ten feet. Oh, take them down. Take the mirrors down. Don't look at me.

Inside the pearl, silver, gray, chrome condo, he couldn't help but brag.

"Terry designed it."

"Huh."

"She designed it herself. 'Cept the sunken living space, that was there first. They're all like that."

"Living space?"

"You know, this here."

Gesturing down to the sofa, glass-top coffee table. Ivory gas fireplace, who is this man? Who is this man in front of me? This can't be my dad. Yes, there's the pickle-nose, a little. Yes, there's the splotchy skin, but the tan, the Tommy Bahama shirt with buttons, the khaki pants? Where the fuck did you come from, man in dad-suit, semi-dad?

"Shauna, have a seat. How 'bout here?"

And now sitting down on the gray-silver sofa, tiny seagulls in silver stitching, just for texture. Everything smelling new, just bought, just-bought slick chrome-and-crystal condo. Where the fuck am I?

"So . . . what brings you to Mount Pleasant?"

"Um."

"New boyfriend?"

Dumb. That was dumb. Shouldn't have said it. Yeah, right. Looking like that. New boyfriend. Maybe Al Roker. Fat Albert.

"You, Dad. I came to talk to you."

"Oh, yeah? Well. I mean. There's a phone here. We do 'have the technology' . . . Wanna drink?"

"Yeah."

Too fast. Yeah, I want a drink too fast. Yesterday even. Yesterday and all the days before.

"What's on your mind? You like Captain Morgan? It's spiced. You gotta try it. Goes great with Coke. Just great."

Mixing up the Captain Morgan spiced rum, oh, to be on the sea. To be away from this landlocked condo complex out on the sea somewhere with Captain Morgan and his parrot and his eye patch and his spiced rum in barrels and away from three-hundred-pound daughters with imploring eyes and nothing to say.

"The ice is the trick. You gotta have the ice."

Ha. That's a laugh. Did you have to have the ice all those years in our crashing-down ash shack back home? Did you have to have the ice in your 10-AM-brown-plastic-gin-and-Coke-or-whatever's-left glass back on Route 31?

Handing Shauna the drink, an assuring smile.

"Bottoms up, kid. Good to see ya."

Good to see you. Already said that, Christ, how many times can I say it without sounding like a jerk-off?

"Dad . . . what happened to you? I mean, what is all this? What . . . is this?"

Silence. Ice clinking. Take sip.

"Shauna, change happens quick. You know, a lot of people sit around and wait, wait for change to happen, to them. But not me. Not after I found Tony."

"What—?"

"Tony Robbins. *Ultimate Power.* That's what it is. It's just ultimate power. You should read it."

Taking it out past the wet bar, a black hardback book with a gleaming cover. A giant of a man smiling from the gloss, big teeth, arms crossed.

"This book changed my life. I want you to have it."

Handing over the gleaming black book to Shauna, a heavy tome, a Bible-black brick. Hope it works. Maybe it will work. God knows she needs it.

Shauna taking the book, a confused pink pudge face, eyes

looking for something to grasp, something to latch onto. Everyone back at Hope was talking about the case, the documentary, the town abuzz with gossip. But here was Dad, hours away, talking about Tony.

"Dad . . . if you did something. If you did something that you know wasn't right . . . even if it was a long time ago—"

"The past is dead, kid. The past's the past. All you got is the future. And . . . " Tapping the book with his forefinger. "The future is now."

"But what if—"

"No excuses."

"But, Dad, listen to me—"

"No excuses, kiddo. The future is what you make it."

And now the door opens, goddammit, and there is Terry. Terry in her peach sarong and swimsuit, gold bracelet.

"Oh."

"Well, hello, Terry. This is Shauna."

Not wanting to say it, not wanting to say it.

"My daughter."

And there she is. Flip-flops in September. Shorts. A muumuu of a shirt, a tent thing with little pink flowers. And that hair. Grease head. Black roots. And into dry, dry wispy breaking blonde frazzle. Rat hair.

"Oh! Well, Shauna, it's nice to meet you. Real nice to meet you. Here, won't you sit down? Want a drink? Oh, what am I saying, you've got a drink. How bout a—"

"It's fine. I'm fine. I was just leaving, actually."

What a relief!

"Oh, so soon . . . "

"Yeah, I gotta get back. I got an early shift, in the morning."

"Hm."

"Yeah, I got a new job, telemarketing. It's okay. I mean, the hours are good."

"Oh. Okay."

"Listen, Dad, it's good to see you."

Good to see you! Good to see you! It's so goddamn good to see everyone around here I could tear my face off!

"Mind if I just . . . use your bathroom before I go…it's a long drive back so . . . "

And Troy standing there like a wooden post, a palm-shirt scarecrow. What do I do?

He wasn't gonna tell her, later. No way he would tell Terry. Later. After Shauna scurried out, polite good-byes all around, pleasantries in turquoise. No, there was no way to tell her, when Terry went back down to the clubhouse, what he found in the bedroom.

There it was, a nice little white note, in front of a nice shiny hardback black book, with a smiling tall man and, on top of it, a heaping pile of human shit. A pile of it.

On the note:

"Dearest father, This is what I think of the past."

"PS: Don't forget to tell Terry to put on the wedding dress and cry while you fuck her."

T W O

A million miles of cable between them, stretched out on a wire.
A system of radio signals, satellite signals, digital symbol in
ones and twos spiraling down to focus, at the Home Depot, the
TV set in the break room, back in Torrance. That's him, isn't it?

Torrance, California, where Jeff Cody had just been pro-
moted to assistant manager. Ah, beautiful Torrance! Where Jeff
Cody had stumbled after years upon years of blowing around,
pissing away time, scorching it, doing whatever it is a man can do
to make his head stop.

Yes, he knew they were coming. Of course they were coming.
They would come and find him, track him down, wheedle their
way into his sidelines, the margins of his shit-ball drive-to-work
days and after-hours, this cockroach life, hiding around and in
between boxes, stacks, piles of wood, burrowing out, only when
the lights off, a thousand little tentacles, crawling scared. What
kind of life is this? A look-back life. A thousand broken light-
bulbs, might-have-beens, a thousand maybe-what-ifs. Junk cars on
the pavement, everything a past glory, a past almost.

Living a life of almost-had-turned, somehow, everything
inward, everything else away. The gang, the boys, all of them,

where now? In Pittsburgh, in Phoenix, in Plano. Gone to the four corners, spread, a common cause of guilt, a mirror unheld. Get them away! Lose them! Put them in boxes, ship them out, stack them high and steep, get them out of here. Storage. Lock the lock, throw away the key.

Those sunny, summer-always sunshine days of Torrance. Don't look at the ground, don't look at the cement. Keep your head up, up and away. Keep your head up to the bright bulb always summer sky, never mind the concrete blocks, barbed wire, metal fences, junkyard gates, rusty trucks, burned-out signs, leaning signposts. Keep your head to the sky, Torrance. And whatever you do . . . don't look back.

That morning he'd meant to take it easy. Don't sweat it, boss. Assistant manager Cody. And assistant manager Cody of the Home Depot didn't sweat it, why should he, that morning in Hardware or Fixtures or Plumbing. There was nothing to sweat. A slow Tuesday morning dragging along. A cleanup on aisle five, in Paint, someone dumped a can of primer. Dumbshit. That was not gonna be easy. Put up the cones. The orange ones. Mojado. Danger. Wet paint.

Slip-n-falls! Christ, the lecture they give 'em on slip-n-falls. Two days devoted to the viscosity of tiles, the treatment, miracle treatment you put on the tiles. MORE traction when wet! MORE traction in the rain! Not that it rained much in sunshine always-happy Torrance. January and February, that's it. The rainy season. In June. June gloom. The blah cloud season. That's the only season. Two months of rain in winter. One month in summer of gloom. The rest, fuck it, sunshine all around. That bright marble blue cloudless sky beating down on iron fencing and padlocks and lectures about slip-n-falls, out on the patio next to the nursery. You can get a hot dog on the truck but I wouldn't eat it. Burritos, too.

The no-papers fenced in, in a cage, waiting to work. Take a number and they'll paint your house practically for free, they'll move you, they'll clean your toilets, they'll mow your lawn, for peanuts, scraps, a shrug. They want to work. Jeff Cody strolling out on Sundays, out to the pen. *Agua! Agua, amigos!* Giving them water in the beating-down sun. Jesus. You had to feel sorry for them. On Christmas he'd given out a bunch of returns in a raffle. No big deal, he couldn't sell them anyway. And beer. *Cervezas! Cervezas, amigos!* It was obvious they were good people, fucking sweat their asses off for four bucks an hour in the beat-down heat. You couldn't help but feel bad for them. What the fuck did they ever do?

And there, in landscaping, between the bougainvillea and the azaleas, in Outdoor Nursery, assistant manager Jeff Cody rounded the corner and stood face-to-face with, eyes to eyes, staring at, Detective Samuel Barnett of the Muskegon, Michigan, police.

Beside him, flanked, a cop of each color, one white bread, one black. Big-bicep-bodied L.A. kind of cops, Rodney King cops, Rampart cops, cops you didn't want to fuck with. Cops not on the beat, cops not on a squad. Cops on a force. Cops like soldiers. City soldiers, armored, billy-clubbed, heat-packed, muscle-bound.

Between them, a relic, Detective Samuel Barnett of fish-town Michigan.

"Jeff Cody, you are under arrest for the murder of Elizabeth Lynn Krause."

And the cuffs get put on.

"Anything you say can and will be held against you in a court of . . . "

And the white cop and the black cop get to lead him through the maiden grass, through the lace-leaf maple, through the crimson queen. The sweet-scent blooms of jasmine, the gentle trellis of periwinkle, gardenia, peonies, poppies, daisies, belles, all watching as the black-beetle uniforms scurry through, marching past the lily-of-the-valley, the ruby stella, the old-fashioned bleeding heart.

And behind them, the law words, the make-it-right Miranda words of halls of marble, justice words float through, through and up toward the bright cobalt sky, a sky made of Play-Doh, banishing clouds to Michigan, banishing gloom to Michigan.

And below, the bougainvillea and the bluebells gossip and giggle. The peonies concur. The poppies demur. And the sweetheart roses smile finally.

THREE

A raw scallop sky in the middle of March, the nothing month. The courthouse, the cement steps, the beige brick walls all faded as a photograph, turning white before your eyes. Blink now and it was never there.

No one knows what to make of this new century, 2004 and it's not looking good. They had come from every corner of Michigan, all parts of the glove, from Holland to Saginaw, from Clarkston to Traverse City. The story had filled them with rage. Gross indifference. Reckless endangerment. Murderers! Animals! Sickos! Some with signs: JUSTICE FOR ELIZABETH! BURN THE BASTARDS! FRY 'EM! And then, the churches . . . from Good Shepherd Assembly to New Hope Bible to the United Methodist down the way. The Dearborn Heights Baptist all the way from Detroit. A candlelight vigil. Prayers in silence. Some pray for clemency. Some pray for revenge. The snow plower and his wife seated at the back of the courtroom, hand in hand. And the students, the classes in Hope College, practically empty. The students down at the courthouse. And for the law students, a required course. A field trip.

And for the four students Danek, Lars, Brad, and Katy—a special seat, there would be the Lt. Colonel and his lovely wife,

Dorothy. Brad and Katy sitting protectively next to the Lt. Colonel. Lars next to Danek next to Dorothy. Danek held fast next to her. He would save her. The couple, quiet, unheeding of the cameras and the gasping and the scrutiny.

And across from this—the defendants.

Seeing how they'd aged, you'd think they'd already been in prison. Billy and Terrance and Randy and Russ. Spread across the states like spores. From Reno to Tampa to Buffalo . . . they'd been rounded up and now reunited. A parade of shame.

And Jeff Cody. Now dyeing his hair, what was left of his hair, brown. A cheap bottle-brown. A Just for Men brown. He couldn't stand it. So this. This! This is how he meets the Lt. Colonel and his wife. Not at Thanksgiving, not at Christmas, not at the wedding to their daughter. But here, in court, twenty-five years later and at the trial for their daughter, his one true love. His one true love whom he strangled. His one true love whom he dumped by the side of the road in the snow. How he wished to explain it! How could he? Impossible. It had all gone through his hands like sugar.

And there she was, Shauna Boggs. The Blob. Piggy-face. There she was in her teal sweater and foofy hair, thinking, how could it be twenty-five years earlier, that grabbing for Jeff at the Green Mill Inn. Afterward. At five in the morning, watching him pack, how could it be that she'd begged him, cried to him, "Don't leave me. Oh, please don't leave me." Acting out a scene from a movie of the week she'd maybe seen earlier or later or maybe just made up. "Don't you see? Now it's just us! It's meant to be." And thinking that Jeff looking up was gonna mean a movie kiss. He loves me! But, instead, he sticks to the wall, sinking into the wood panel and gritting his teeth.

Seeing her then, a glob of want. What he would give to switch back. What he would give to reverse it. "Don't you get it? It's over." And wanting to chop up time and throw her in the woods instead. Why couldn't it have been her? He'd been had. Not enough pills to turn it back, never enough pills anymore. Falling now, melting into the ground. Now, collapsing into the floor, a whimper, a slop of remorse. "I'm dead. I'm just fucking dead." A man turned boy in the carpet. Shauna looking down, quick, now she has him. Reaching her hand to his neck, to console him. Before she touches him, he freezes, "Stop it. You'll never be her, pig-face."

Shauna Boggs now. Not able to look at him, or across the aisle, not able to keep her head on her neck. Not able to meet the eyes of the coroner, those damning words, "Yes, that's correct. DNA evidence. Saliva. Female. Matching the defendant." And then the realization, a wave through the court. She'd spat on her. Shauna Boggs had spat on her best friend while she lay pummeled on the floor. A hush. Hatred heavy as a house.

Shauna Boggs, the last name read off. The last conviction. All of them. Homicide. Abduction. Murder. Aggravated assault. Assault with a deadly weapon. Assault and battery. Gross indifference. Conspiracy to commit murder. The myriad names for it. The many names for what happened that night. Who knew what happened that night had so many names? And that's how she saw it. Not what they did. Not what she did. What happened.

She had not meant to catch eyes with anyone and particularly not with Dotsy. But there she was, looking at her, or through her, from across the courtroom. She had looked away. Not fast enough. But now, in Shauna's head, a thousand rushing thoughts, a tsunami, almost she couldn't hear it, when they read it, now, over the din.

Shauna Boggs. Conspiracy to commit murder. Gross indifference. Murder one.

Listen to it. You'll hear it for days. You'll hear it for the rest of your life in a gray little box. Shauna Boggs, the State of Michigan hereby sentences you to . . . drum roll please . . . life in prison. Sentence to be served immediately. No parole.

A hammer to the head. A shock to the system. What they did that night. What she did. No longer what happened.

And Detective Samuel Barnett standing at the back of the courtroom. Mister Perfect. For him, an almost smile. A quiver of a smile from Shauna to him through the glass, eyes welling up. A wink. She throws him the thought through that red-eye wink. She throws him the thought and it lands on him, catch.

It was her.

She was the one who had given up the dingy little box.

The Polaroids.

She was the one who had left the box at the station.

She had given herself up.

FOUR

It would be strange, at the end of your life, measuring it out, teaspoon by teaspoon; what did you get?

Who would forgive you? And would you forgive yourself? All of your indiscretions—were you a fool? Maybe you were just a whore, after all. Or a weather vane, aimless and choking, always choking in gust after gust, tumult after tumult . . . what did you make of it?

Shauna sat there, in her ash-by-ash little box, staring at the wall, thinking of that moment, centuries ago, when she had not been Shauna Blobs, then Blobs, then Blob, when she had said, "Good." When her friend, not best friend, not dearest friend, but most precious friend, had been ushered into heaven? She had even laughed.

Laughed.

How much biting, eating away, crumbling into herself, doughnuts and Twinkies and Pop-Tarts, too. How much gorging after gorging, throwing up, then gorging again. Looking at herself, wanting to throw up again, endlessly, eternally, 'til the end of time?

And when she shuffled off this too-sullied body, when she left the Blob behind and flew up, straight on a wire . . . would she then shortly descend? Or had she already descended?

It wasn't that she was going mad, exactly. It was just . . . there were whispers. Tiny ones. Little voices, coming quick like ambush thoughts. They will see me. They will kill me. They are trying to kill me here. They will laugh at me. They are laughing at me. They have always been laughing at me. I'm not safe. I'm not safe here. I'm not safe here through the night. Rapier voices, slashing in and out and back into the temple, sometimes from the back of the skull. Don't you see? It's over.

They will get me.

FIVE

There beside the lake, two black spindle trees, one out-stretched upward reaching high into the infinite dusk, the other crumpled in on itself, crying into its belly, hobbled. And there, on the bench between, a raven woman. Dotsy Krause. An almost-painter with memories in brushstrokes of the Lindy Hop at the Three Deuces, of a sweltering July spent in Cape Cod, of a Wedgwood locket found and lost. Each brushstroke a pulse, the shock of it a kind of vista disappearing into the horizon, once it was there, then smaller and smaller, then minuscule, then a pinprick, then nothing.

The Lt. Colonel didn't know she would come here, wouldn't like it. But there had to be something. Looking down, seeing the hands attached to her wrists shaking. More frequent now, and stronger. Last week she had even dropped a teacup. Irreplaceable. He had brought it back from Seoul.

There must be something. A cure somehow in the wind off the dunes.

Looking out across the pitch-gloam water, as fixed as glass, Dorothy Krause had the feeling of being watched. And for a moment, above her, as she peered over into the gloom-glass lake, that still-ice Michigan, never-light water, she thought she saw, but no, how could she . . . a rustle of light, a ghost figure, a tentative quiver. And a whisper came quick, almost from the trees . . . take me back gently, into the night sky.

I will wait for you.

And Dotsy, hearing her daughter's voice, turns in pieces to the green pine trees, searching desperate in grasps and shadows, through the elm, through the elder, through the oaks. And then realizing, yes, of course, there was no one there and never would be again.

SIX

The green blades of the tulips stabbing up through the dirt like half-buried knives. It had rained for two days straight, but now the sun shining over the puddles, turning dew into diamonds on the Kelly grass spears. The sun back, reassuring, never-mind, never-mind, I am here. I came back.

Dotsy hadn't known what to wear to the Kent County Correctional Facility, Holton, Michigan. She had never been, nor thought she would ever be, in such a place, and she, well, she didn't think she'd be back. Wondering, as she stepped out of the green striped taxi onto the dew-sheathed sidewalk . . . will I be back? And then deciding, No. No, I won't.

A grid. All around a grid. Squares and rectangles, laid out in gray. And, too, a barbwire frame.

There was no reason to be here. No one knew she was coming anyway, certainly not her husband. Of course not. She could leave at any moment. No one would know.

Through, through, through each door, each gate, each cage, chain metal corridors clanking open and shut. Open and shut. Locking you out, locking you in.

Dotsy descending somehow, each circle down into the next,

into a drab dishwater room, ammonia-laced. Scrubbed, scrubbed, scrubbed erasing all sins, the walls whispering regret. Take me home.

All that was required was to turn around. Turn around and this will all be over. Twenty-five years of this and still not over. These gray circles, this dust-mop cage, this the only way to make it stop.

She was alone but it was not special treatment. She was alone because it was Tuesday at two and these people have to work for God's sake. Worker class. Work or prison. You choose.

Shauna had not been expecting a visitor. Ever. And maybe that was why, over these last few months, she had the expression of a lost rabbit down the watering hole. Oh, this room, yes. This room I had not seen. This was a room for people with families. Moms. Daughters. Baby girls. Grandsons. Little boys. Fathers. Husbands. No, this room was not for me.

And yet, there across the gunmetal concrete, Dotsy sat in a chair. Comical. A woman of her age. A woman in pearls with a purse . . . here. Some sort of comedy sketch with no punch line. But then, Shauna thought, oh, yes, the punch line is me.

She had lost weight. It's not that Dotsy had ever thought about Shauna Boggs's snickering obesity, although she'd overheard the taunts. Sometimes, after the verdict, to make her feel better, the derision was proffered to her like an ice-cream cone. Eat up. We'll make fun. That's what we'll do. But it did not make her feel better, any more than vultures eating carrion by the side of the road would make her feel better. Dotsy could see nothing but the carrion.

And so Shauna was plump now. Simply plump. No longer obese. And inside that face, somewhere, were the vestiges of that little girl who'd come over to play Candy Land, to play hopscotch, to call boys. She had worn a black one-piece swimsuit as a halter top. Dotsy did remember that. Thinking at the time, cover up! Cover up, they'll get you!

Shauna doesn't look at her when she sits down, or ever, for that matter. Shauna keeps her eyes strained on the table, the chairs, the floor. Anything other than her. Her, here. The mother.

And there is a kind of quiet made of feeling giddy or being in love or finding home. But this is not that quiet. This is a quiet of failure, of wanting to go back, of restlessness.

Figuring out that she's the only one who will be speaking. Figuring out that maybe this is stupid and she should just go home in the first place, never should have come. Dotsy tries to keep her hands from shaking, but they shake now, little tremors, all day long. Barely able to write her name, or make out a check. Good thing she's not still painting. Trembling hands, hold each other on the table. Hold still.

The guard gives her a nod, better hurry up, you're on the clock. This is not the country club. Well, of course not. Isn't that obvious? This is the place you get to go to if you'll never make it to the country club. Lucky bastards, they have no idea.

Okay, break this moment. This silence deafening, make it stop. "Shauna."

And there it is, her name. Gentle. Spoken in a way it had not been spoken for years. Spoken like she was a person.

But still, there is no looking up. Shauna's eyes fixed on the floor, blinded.

"Shauna, I can't carry this. Um. I can't carry this any longer."

Expecting a reaction. What was she expecting? Tears? Revelation? Laughter? Whatever it was she had been expecting, here there was nothing. Here there were just eyes fixed on metal chairs.

Another try. Get in. Look at me, Shauna.

"I was in love, once, you know."

Maybe there is something there in Shauna now, something stirring, but still, eyes stay staring at the steel square tiles.

"It was a kind of madness. Like trying to pour an ocean into a teacup. Funny. All it could do was spill and break." And then a kind of laugh, stifled.

Maybe this will make her eyes get off the tile. Look here. Look at me. But no, not even this. She is gone now, isn't she?

And noticing now, for the first time, on the side of her face, a scar, four inches long, but deep, just healing. Just missed her eye. Christ, what had they done to her? What happens here? What happens here in this horrible place? This place made of nightmares, contract-built. A kind of slavery for being poor. A kind of slavery for mistakes, if you're poor. But no, they are here for a reason, Dotsy told herself. They are here for a reason. Aren't they?

Trembling hands reaching now, fumbling into the coral clip purse, an envelope-looking thing, subtle as a shoe shine. But elegant, look closer. Mother-of-pearl on the clasp. Look closer. Meticulous.

And out comes the locket. That blue silhouette cameo from days on the sound, days in the water playing stupid seashell games with Edward. That salty blue cameo from days on the levee, from days with Jeff Cody, from days on the ground.

"Have it, Shauna."

And then, somehow a breath, "I want you to have it."

If she'd been able to look up from the gray tile floor, look up from the grid of gray-laced white speckles, she would have. She would have lifted her eyes and met Dotsy's and then maybe there would have been tears. Of what? Gratitude? Desperation? Regret?

But, no, there was no looking up. There couldn't be. As easily as packing the sun into a basket. As easily as killing the moon. That's how easy that could be. No, there was no looking up. It was impossible. Now.

The locket now just sitting there on the table. A dumb gift. A gesture stalled. Dotsy almost wanting to take it back now. Maybe this was ridiculous.

But no. There's no want in a gift. There can be no taking in a gift. And anyway, this isn't giving. Any more than the ocean gives to the tide. Let these waters crash in out, in out, taking this burden out to sea. Someday the sand will whisper this.

The guard, nodding again, time's up. And that is that. Do it quick, do it fast, get out of here. You don't belong here, lady, in the land of zombies and miscues and never-beens. Out of here, sweet old lady, go home and bake cookies. This is not a place for you.

And Dotsy, one last look at Shauna. Strange, how she felt sorry for her, considering. Strange, how she wanted to hold her, to soften her, to comfort her, considering.

But now, with the gate and the alarm and the gray metal clanking her out, out into the bright blue sky, out into the gorgeous green glass globe, she was lighter. Dotsy was lifted, as if on a wire, twenty-five years later and now somehow not touching the ground. Out there the sky could be blue again, out there the clouds could be puff-puff-puffy like cotton candy. Out there the smell of grass and the breeze off the lake, all these things could contrive to make happy. As simple as a clock ticking. As simple as the sound of the rain.

And inside now. Shauna standing at the gate, waiting for the electric door. The alarm will go off, so loud it scares you. Every time it scares you. Shauna Boggs, staring into the gate, past the gate, down down down into the maze upon maze, the rat-maze of choices and bad choices and missteps, in degrees of gray, charcoal, dust, endless and banning. Shauna Boggs walking by the guards, past the guards, some nodding tiny, some looking away, looking through, looking through her. Shauna Boggs, walking past the guards, quietly steeling herself, wondering which one of them will find her feet swinging in the morning light.

ACKNOWLEDGMENTS

Obviously, this wouldn't be possible without the help, support and advice from some very kind people. (Otherwise I would just be babbling to myself in a room somewhere.) So here goes . . . Thank you to my amazing mother and best friend, Nancy Portes Kuhnel. My whole family, Charles, Lisa, Alejandro Portes, Pats, Doug, Nancy, Bobby and Carlos. My grandparents: Lt. Colonel Charles Brazie & Arlene Brazie. Helio & Eulalia Portes. The gentleman who keeps me sane: Brad Kluck. My dear friends: Dawn Cody, Mira Crisp, Simon Eldon-Edington, Matthew Specktor, Natasha Leggero, Io Perry, Noelle Hale, Super A, Gary Wishik, Tylene De Vine, Demetrius Griffin, Amy Stokes, Niels Alpert, Jenniefer Pacelli and Haley Gore. My editor, Dan Smetanka. (Thanks for taking a chance on me.) My literary agent, Katie Shea at Donald Mass Literary Agency. My book-to-film agent, Josie Freedman at ICM. Everyone at Soft Skull. Fred Ramey at Unbridled Books, my editor on HICK. Kristen Pettit at HarperCollins, my editor on ANATOMY OF A MISFIT. Everyone involved in HICK the film: Derick Martini, Chloe Grace Moretz, Eddie Redmayne, Blake Lively, Charles de Portes, Alec Baldwin, Juliette Lewis, Rory Culkin, Christian Taylor, Ray McKinnon, Teri and Trevor

Moretz, Jon "Peepaw" Cornick, Erica Munro, Roshelle Berliner, Frank Godwin, Michael Jefferson, Pedro Portes and Tommy Brazie. Finally, I'd like to thank the one and only little prince, my sun and moon and stars, my baby boy: Wyatt Storm.